GUNBOAT BARRAGE!

It was no time to be choosy. There was only one boat available. The Black Eagle detachment crowded aboard as Falconi pushed forward on the throttle and cranked the wheel. The launch wheeled in the water, throwing out a wild wake, and headed for the middle of the river.

But all hopes were dashed when three NVA boats, machine guns blazing, swept out to intercept them. Big 12.7 millimeter rounds smacked, splattered and rocked the Black Eagle team's craft, slapping gaping holes into the gunwales and across the foredeck. Suddenly the control console exploded in Falconi's face as a half dozen of the big slugs blasted it apart.

From all appearances, the Battle of Tam Nuroc was over—and the defeat promised watery graves for the Black Eagles!

BLACK EAGLES
by John Lansing

They're the best jungle fighters the United States has to offer. No matter where Charlie is hiding, The Eagles will find him! They're the greatest unsung heroes of the dirtiest, most challenging war of all time!

DUEL ON THE SONG CAI

THE BLACK EAGLES #11

ZEBRA BOOKS
KENSINGTON PUBLISHING CORP.

Special acknowledgement to Patrick E. Andrews

ZEBRA BOOKS

are published by

Kensington Publishing Corp.
475 Park Avenue South
New York, NY 10016

First printing: April 1987

Printed in the United States of America

Dedicated to
The 5th Armored Division
"The Victory Division"

THE BLACK EAGLES ROLL OF HONOR

(Assigned or Attached Personnel Killed in Action)

Sergeant Barker, Toby — U.S. Marine Corps
Sergeant Barthe, Eddie — U.S. Army
Sergeant Bernstein, Jacob — U.S. Marine Corps
First Lieutenant Blum, Marc — U.S. Air Force
Sergeant Boudreau, Marcel — U.S. Army
Sergeant Carter, Demond — U.S. Army
Master Sergeant Chun, Kim — South Korean Marines
Staff Sergeant Dayton, Marvin — U.S. Army
Sergeant First Class Galchaser, Jack — U.S. Army
Sergeant Hodges, Trent — U.S. Army
Mister Hosteins, Bruno — ex-French Foreign Legion
Petty Officer Second Class Jackson, Fred — U.S. Navy
Chief Petty Officer Jenkins, Claud — U.S. Navy
Specialist Four Laird, Douglas — U.S. Army
Sergeant Limo, Raymond — U.S. Army
Petty Officer Third Class Littleton, Michael — U.S. Navy
Lieutenant Martin, Buzz — U.S. Navy
Petty Officer Second Class Martin, Durwood — U.S. Navy
Staff Sergeant Maywood, Dennis — U.S. Army
Sergeant First Class Miskoski, Jan — U.S. Army
Staff Sergeant Newcomb, Thomas — Australian Army
First Lieutenant Nguyen Van Dow — South Vietnamese Army
Staff Sergeant O'Quinn, Liam — U.S. Marine Corps
Sergeant First Class Ormond, Norman — U.S. Army
Sergeant Park, Chun Ri — South Korean Marines
Sergeant First Class Rivera, Manuel — U.S. Army
Master Sergeant Snow, John — U.S. Army
Staff Sergeant Taylor, William — Australian Army
Lieutenant Thompson, William — U.S. Navy
Staff Sergeant Tripper, Charles — U.S. Army
First Lieutenant Wakely, Richard — U.S. Army
Staff Sergeant Whitaker, George — Australian Army
Gunnery Sergeant White, Jackson — U.S. Marine Corps

ROSTER OF THE BLACK EAGLES
(Operation Song Cai)

COMMAND ELEMENT

Lieutenant Colonel Robert Falconi
U.S. Army
Commanding Officer
(10 Black Eagle Missions)

Chief Petty Officer Leland Brewster
U.S. Navy
Communications Chief
(1 Black Eagle Mission)

Corporal Archie Dobbs
U.S. Army
Detachment Scout
(8 Black Eagle Missions)

FIRE TEAM ALPHA

Lieutenant Chris Hawkins
U.S. Navy
Team Leader/Exec. Officer
(1 Black Eagle Mission)

Master Sergeant Ray Swift Elk
U.S. Army
Auto Rifleman/Intelligence
(3 Black Eagle Missions)

Staff Sergeant Paulo Garcia
U.S. Marine Corps
Grenadier
(Newly Assigned)

Staff Sergeant Enrique Valverde
U.S. Army
Rifleman/Supply
(1 Black Eagle Mission)

FIRE TEAM BRAVO

Sergeant Major Duncan Gordon
U.S. Army
Team Leader/Operations
(8 Black Eagle Missions)

Sergeant First Class Malcomb McCorckel
U.S. Army
Auto Rifleman/Medic
(9 Black Eagle Missions)

Sergeant First Class Calvin Culpepper
U.S. Army
Grenadier
(9 Black Eagle Missions)

Petty Officer Third Class Blue Richards
U.S. Navy
Rifleman
(3 Black Eagle Missions)

PROLOGUE

The small hamlet of Tam Nuroc was nestled on a curving bank of the Song Cai River. Breezes, cooled by the water, made it a lush, refreshing oasis in the steaming jungle. The village huts, situated in a palm grove, were twenty meters from the river itself. A small dock, constructed of lashed tree logs, projected out into deeper water so that even large boats that traveled the waterway could tie up there during visits to the little town.

Tam Nuroc had always been primarily a market place. Countless generations of Vietnamese country people gathered there for animated bargaining, important meetings, politics and social events. Trading, selling, employment opportunities, and even arrangements of marriages had flourished in the village square for as long as anyone could remember.

But for a period of time, Tam Nuroc played a different role. It still served as a central meeting place, but the friendliness and joviality were no longer in evidence during those long months. The villagers became members of a self-defense militia who were forced to turn to weapons in order to

11

defend themselves against attacks of the Viet Cong.

When the Communists established themselves in the area, they could not tolerate such displays of free enterprise in the countryside. Particularly if it actually benefited everyone concerned. After several murderous raids on their village by the Viet Cong, the people had turned to the government for help. A cadre of officers and sergeants was dispatched to organize a militia comprised of the village's men. An effective training program, and American supplied equipment, produced a force strong enough to not only resist the Red encroachment into the people's lives, but to actually defeat the local Viet Cong outfit, and rid the countryside of the dangerous pests.

But the victory and the two years of peace that followed eventually made the villagers complacent. Then, unfortunately, things came to a head during the big market day that celebrated the holiday of the Feast of Doan Ngo.

The river bank was packed with people, their customary dealings carried out in a loud combination of chattering and laughter. The sound of the approaching patrol boat scarcely attracted their attention. ARVN river units frequently called on Tam Nuroc during these occasions so the men could buy food to supplement their rations.

An old man, standing behind his boiling pot of noodle soup, anxiously waited for the soldiers to come ashore. They always purchased canteen cups of his delicacy, and paid good piasters for it too. But something troubled him as he watched the boat ease toward the shore. The men in it were military, no doubt, but the two heavy machine guns mounted on the flying bridge were aimed straight into the throng of people.

Then he saw the red stars on the gunners' pith helmets.

Before the oldster could shout an alarm, the automatic weapons kicked into action. The slugs sprayed into the compact crowd, crashing into the marketeers and mowing them down in screaming packs. Confused and panic-stricken, they ran aimlessly in the hail of steel-jacketed 7.62 millimeter slugs that slammed into their bodies.

The killing went on for fifteen minutes, and included two reloads of 250-round belts, before the boat's motor was thrown into reverse. The coxswain backed the craft out into deeper water, then turned the bow toward the north. He hit the throttles hard, and roared back up the river.

The days of peace were gone, not only for Tam Nuroc, but for the whole of the Song Cai River.

CHAPTER 1

It was only mid-morning, but the sun was already a blazing disk in the pale, cloudless sky over the Special Forces B Team camp of Nui Dep. The temperature had streaked upward to over a hundred degrees, and the steamy humidity added to the torrid weather that sapped the strength of the fortified hamlet's population.

Two shirtless men, their fatigue trousers crammed into the top of their unlaced boots, lugged a large G.I. garbage pail full of crushed beer cans to a deep sump. The sweat streamed down their faces and glistened on their torsos as they upended the container into the trash hole not far from the bunker they called home. The discomfort that was so evident in their faces was not as much from the uncomfortable weather—they were used to that—but more from the monstrous hangovers that pounded in their heads.

The two were Malpractice McCorckel and Calvin Culpepper from the Black Eagle Detachment that was billeted in the camp. Their unit had spent the entire previous night celebrating three promotions—and one demotion—by stuffing themselves on roast

15

pork and washing it down with gallons of beer. The latter was also augmented with generous shots of scotch and bourbon.

The commanding officer, Robert Falconi, had been upped from the rank of major to lieutenant colonel. To add to the glad tidings, the two senior non-coms also added a rocker and star to their respective uniform sleeves. Top Gordon, the operations sergeant, went from master sergeant E-8 to sergeant major E-9. The intelligence sergeant, a full-blooded Sioux Indian named Ray Swift Elk, was made a master sergeant E-8 from the rank of sergeant first class E-7. Like several other members of the Black Eagles, they wore two hats: Top also led Fire Team Bravo, and Swift Elk was the automatic rifleman of Fire Team Alpha, and was also the assistant team leader of that fine group of men.

Their promotions were well-deserved, and their new chevrons were properly wetted down amid congratulations and wishes for continued good luck in the army.

Archie Dobbs, on the other hand, was a completely different story.

He served as the detachment scout and had been diligently performing his duties in the grade of staff sergeant. But he ran into a bit of a problem on the last operation his detachment participated in. During the infiltration parachute jump, Archie's main chute failed to deploy properly and he rode the malfunction all the way into the ground. He suffered a severe concussion and internal injuries. He was evacuated from the field to an army hospital at Long Binh, where he exhibited a quick recovery. His noble requests to return to his unit were turned down, so he went AWOL to rejoin the Black Eagles. Despite the fact he'd actually gone back into combat, he was

16

reduced from staff sergeant to corporal at the insistence of the hospital commanding officer. The medical officer said he'd be damned if any sonofabitch was going to take unauthorized leave from his unit, and he didn't care where the malefactor went. Back to battle was the same as downtown Saigon as far as he was concerned. Since he was right—by the book at least—and the Black Eagles were part of a clandestine echelon that had to avoid publicity or other exposure, no one was able to fight the charges.

Archie, who had run up and down the rank ladder a number of times anyway, wasn't really upset by the situation. Particularly when his stay under military medical care had resulted in his gaining a special friend of the feminine persuasion. His sweetheart, a nurse named 2nd Lt. Betty Lou Pemberton, had helped him escape the hard clutches of medical corps bureaucracy and get back to the field.

He had also been able to have a few *liaisons d'amour* with her right there at Nui Dep when she'd come out with a special clinic team to provide medical care and examinations to the camp's civilian population. Their final parting, two nights before, had been as passionate as it was loving.

Thoughts of Betty Lou eased the pain of losing rank, so at the party the previous night, Archie simply grinned, popped open another can of beer, and went to his locker to dig among his uniforms which bore various insignias of grade between PFC and staff sergeant. He finally found a jacket with the two chevrons of corporal, and slipped into it.

"C'est la guerre, what the hell?" said Archie. He chug-a-lugged the beer and got another one. Then he laughed out loud as his mind filled with pictures of Betty Lou and her more than ample bosom. *"C'est la guerre*, hell! *C'est l'amour!"*

17

His detachment pals, as adaptable a group as ever soldiered on God's green earth, appreciated his attitude. So they toasted his *de*motion with the same fervor they saluted the others' *pro*motion.

At any rate, it was a hell of a good party.

Now Malpractice and Calvin returned to the bunker with the emptied garbage can. The Black Eagles had their own quarters located off to one side in the "slums" of the camp. Despite their exposed site (open as much to incoming VC rounds as the blistering weather) the interior of their rather spacious abode was close to luxurious. Their supply sergeant, an enterprising Chicano by the name of Hank Valverde, had been assigned to the detachment prior to their last mission. He'd shown up with fancy furniture, chairs, hospital-style beds, and even a refrigerator.

Top Gordon, an electric fan blowing on him, gazed sleepily at the two other's entrance. "Is that sump filled up yet?" he asked sleepily.

"No, Top," Malpractice answered. As the team medic he was responsible for the sanitary conditions of the unit. "We got almost a week before we gotta cover it up and dig another."

"There ain't nothing in there but beer cans anyhow," Calvin Culpepper said. He walked across the bunker and climbed onto his bed, switching on his own fan. "The way the guys eat around here, we don't never have any garbage to dump in it."

Ray Swift Elk opened his eyes and gazed sleepily over at Calvin. "Hey, Buffalo Soljer, you mean the way *you* eat."

Calvin smiled. "A growing boy got to have his chow."

Swift Elk laughed. "Thirty years old with thirteen years in the goddamned army and he still calls himself a boy."

18

"I'm the eternal youth, Injun," Calvin said.

Top, sleepy and irritable, growled at them. "You two—"

The field telephone on the desk clacked a couple of times. Malpractice, the only man on his feet, walked over and answered it. "Falconi's bunker, Sergeant McCorckel speaking, sir," he pronounced in a correct, crisp military style.

Maj. Rory Riley, the Special Forces officer who commanded Camp Nui Dep's B-Detachment, spoke on the other end. "Gimme Falconi—whoops! Maybe I should say, 'Give Major Riley's compliments to the colonel and tell him I need to speak to him.' "

Malpractice glanced over in the corner where Falconi had established his desk and bed. "He's asleep."

"Wake the sonofabitch up!" Riley yelled into the phone.

"Jesus! Okay, sir," Malpractice said.

But the new lieutenant colonel was awake. Falconi sat up on his bed. "Is that for me?"

"Yeah," Malpractice said. "Riley wants to talk to you."

Falconi, wearing only OD shorts, padded across the bunker's board floor in his bare feet. He took the phone. "What's up, Riley?"

"I hope I ain't disturbing you, *sir*," Riley said. "I'd just fucking die if I thought for one minute that I was a bother, *sir*. I wouldn't—"

"Shut up, Riley," Falconi snarled. "Unless you got something important to say, that is."

"Yes, *sir*! My commo sergeant got a coded message that your everloving boy Fagin is coming out to see you," Riley said. "He'll be coming in by chopper within the hour. Would the colonel like for me to trot out a brass band for the occasion?"

19

"Riley?"

"Yeah, Falconi?"

"Fuck you very much." Falconi hung up the phone and turned to the nine other men in the room. "Fagin's coming in."

They all knew what that meant, but Archie Dobbs summed it up in a three-word understatement:

"Another frigging mission."

Camp Nui Dep had an air strip but could not boast of a control tower to supervise the comings and goings of the various aircraft that visited there. It would have been a big waste of time and energy to have built a structure tall enough to qualify as a normal type of tower. This was because the hamlet was located in a "hot" area that crawled with Viet Cong.

Attacks three or four times a week were the norm, and even a quickly set up Red mortar would have knocked down any towers without much trouble. So the air traffic controller sweltered in a small bunker that boasted a sheet-iron roof complete with sand-bags. Incoming aircraft simply radioed in their ETAs (Estimated Times of Arrival), and the man in the air strip's hole gave them two bits of information: 1) the proper azimuth to come in on, and 2) whether the area was free from incoming enemy rounds or not.

The two helicopters that now approached the camp had been given an all-clear. One, a lumbering H34, was followed by a smaller helicopter that darted around in a restless manner as if looking for something interesting to shoot at. This was an AH-1G Huey Cobra gunship and it was fully armed.

The entire Black Eagle Detachment was standing at the airstrip when the two came in for a roaring, dust-

20

kicking landing. A pre-picked supply detail under Hank Valverde's supervision immediately dashed toward the H34 to pull off the supply requisition that had arraived with the chopper. There were two passengers aboard. The first out was a husky CIA operative named Chuck Fagin. The second was a swarthy Marine staff sergeant. They leaped out of the aircraft and hurried through the swirling clouds of dirt to join Lt. Col. Robert Falconi where he stood with Chris Hawkins and Top Gordon.

Fagin held out his hand. "Congratulations on the promotion."

"Thanks," Falconi said shaking with the arrivee.

Fagin nodded to Top. "You too, Sergeant Major."

Top ignored the remark, looking directly at the other man. "You're Garcia?"

"Yeah," Garcia said. He glanced around. "This is home, huh?"

"Yeah," Top said. "It's where we live between missions." He pointed at the Cobra. "Is that for us?"

"Sure is," Fagin said. "And it's an old friend who's flying it."

The Cobra's rotors stopped spinning, and two men got out. The front cockpit, where the gunner sits, had been occupied by a husky young specialist fourth grade. The pilot got out of his "office" located directly behind and grinned widely at the Black Eagles. This was CW/O Erick Stensland who had flown a completely unauthorized fire support mission for the Black Eagles on the last outing. "How do you guys like my new ship?" he asked walking toward them. His gunner followed.

"Beautiful!" said Archie Dobbs. "Nice to see you again, Erick."

"Same here, Archie," Stensland said. He shook hands around with all the guys. "I'd like you to meet my gunner Gunnar Olson."

"Gunnar the Gunner?" Blue Richards asked.

The young guy, as blond and blue-eyed as Stensland, nodded shyly.

"He's from my hometown," Erickson said. "Knee Lake, Minnesota. We're all shirt-tail relatives there, so Gunnar is probably a cousin to me or something."

Calvin Culpepper squinted his eyes to stare at the design painted on the cowling of the helicopter. "What's that you got up there, Erick?"

"It's a Viking maiden," Erick said. "Gunnar and I are Norwegians, and our ship is called the Naughty Norksi."

"I hope you're here for us," Malpractice McCorckel said. "You sure as hell came in handy the last time."

"Hey!" Archie protested. "I was flying shotgun."

Stensland laughed. "And you did a hell of a fine job, Archie. But I can tell you guys for sure, that Gunnar here is the best damned gunner I've run across yet. And I'm not just saying that because we're related."

Top, with Garcia beside him, interrupted the conversation. "I want you guys to say howdy to the new man. This here's Paulo Garcia, the U.S. Marine Corps' donation to the Black Eagles."

There was another round of handshaking. "Another Chicano, huh?" Ray Swift Elk said. "You can keep ol' Valverde company."

Garcia shook his head. "I'm Portuguese—by way of San Diego. The name is pronounced *Garsha* not *Garseeyah*."

By that time Valverde had joined them after seeing to it that the new supplies had been properly loaded aboard a three-quarter ton truck for the trip over to the bunker. This was cause for another introduction and Hank also shook hands with Gunnar the Gunner

22

Olson and Paulo Garcia.

An animated conversation just began to get underway when the detachment brass—Falconi and Chris Hawkins—joined the group. The colonel had just exchanged a few quick, but important, words with Chuck Fagin. "Let's get over to the house," he said.

No one was surprised that things were starting to move. Fagin showed up among them on only two occasions: at the end of a mission, and at the beginning.

Archie Dobbs noted the canvas OD briefcase under the CIA man's arm. "Whatcha got in there, Chuck? Wouldn't be an operations order, would it?"

"You win the cigar, Archie," Fagin replied. "It most assuredly is a big, fat OPORD."

"What adventures do you have planned for us now, Chuck?" Ray Swift Elk asked. "An assassination in Monaco? Maybe a beach assault on the Riviera?"

"Hey," Blue Richards exlaimed. "How's about a amphibious operation in the Florida Keys? They'se good fishing there, boy!"

Fagin smiled and patted his case. "The answer to your future activity is all in here, boys." He leered at them. "And you ain't gonna like it one bit."

CHAPTER 2

The Black Eagles were the brainchild of a Central Intelligence Agency case officer named Clayton Andrews.

In those early days of the 1960s, Andrews had been doing his own bit of clandestine fighting in Southeast Asia which involved more than harassment missions in Viet Cong areas. His main job was the conduct of operations into North Vietnam itself. When this dangerous assignment was expanded, Andrews began an extensive search for an officer to lead a special detachment he needed to carry out certain down-and-dirty missions. After hundreds of investigations and interviews, he settled on a Special Forces captain named Robert Falconi.

Pulling all the strings he had, Andrews saw to it that the Green Beret officer was transferred to his own branch of SOG—the Special Operations Group—to begin work on a brand new project.

Captain Falconi was tasked with organizing a new fighting unit to be known as the Black Eagles. This group's basic policy was to be primitive and simple: Kill or be killed!

Their mission was to penetrate deep into the heartland of the Communists to disrupt, destroy, maim and slay. The men who would belong to the Black Eagles would be volunteers from every branch of the armed forces. And that was to include all nationalities involved in the struggle against the Red invasion of South Vietnam.

Each man was to be an absolute master in his particular brand of military mayhem. He had to be an expert in not only his own nation's firearms but also those of other friendly and enemy countries. But the required knowledge in weaponry didn't stop at the modern ones. This also included knives, bludgeons, garrotes, and even crossbows when the need to deal silent death had arisen.

There was also a requirement for the more sophisticated and peaceful skills, too. Foreign languages, land navigation, communications, medical and even mountaineering and scuba diving were to be within the realm of knowledge of the Black Eagles. Then, in addition, each man had to know how to type. In an outfit that had no clerks, this office skill was extremely important because they had to do their own paperwork. Much of this was operations orders that directed their dangerous missions. These documents had to be legible and easy to read in order to avoid confusing, deadly errors out in combat.

They became the enforcement arm of SOG, drawing the missions which were the most dangerous and sensitive. In essence they were hit men, closely coordinated and completely dedicated, held together and directed through the forceful personality of their leader, Capt. Robert Falconi.

After Clayton Andrews was promoted out of the job, a new CIA officer moved in. This was Chuck

Fagin. An ex-paratrooper and veteran of both World War II and the Korean War, Fagin had a natural talent when it came to dreaming up nasty things to do to the unfriendlies up north. It didn't take him long to get Falconi and his boys busy.

Their first efforts had been directed against a pleasure palace in North Vietnam. This bordello *par excellence* was used by Communist officials during their retreat from the trials and tribulations of administering authority and regulation over their slave populations. There were no excesses, perverted tastes or unusual demands that went unsatisfied in this hidden fleshpot.

Falconi and his wrecking crew sky-dived into the operational area in a HALO (High Altitude Low Opening) infiltration, and when the Black Eagles finished their raid on the whorehouse, there was hardly a soul left alive to continue the debauchery.

Their next hell-trek into the enemy's hinterlands was an even more dangerous assignment with the difficulty factor multiplied by the special demands placed on them. The North Vietnamese had set up a special prison camp in which they were perfecting their skills in the torture-interrogation of downed American pilots. With the conflict in Southeast Asia, they rightly predicted they would soon have more than a few Yanks in their hands. A North Korean brainwashing expert had come over from his native country to teach them the fine points of mental torment. He had learned his despicable trade during the Korean War when he had American POWs directly under his control. His use of psychological torture, combined with just the right amount of physical torment, had broken more than one man despite the most spirited resistance. Experts who studied his methods came to the conclusion that only a completely insane prisoner could have resisted the North Korean's methods.

At the time of the Black Eagles' infiltration into North Vietnam, the prisoners behind the barbed wire were few, but important. A U.S.A.F. pilot, an Army Special Forces sergeant, and two high-ranking officers of the South Vietnamese forces were the unwilling tenants of the concentration camp.

Falconi and his men were not only assigned to rescue the POWs but also had to bring along the prison's commandant and his North Korean tutor. Falconi pulled the job off, fighting his way south through the North Vietnamese Army and Air Force to a bloody showdown on the Song Bo River. The situation deteriorated to the point that the Black Eagles' magazines had their last few rounds in them as they waited for the NVA's final charge.

The next operation took them to Laos where they were pitted against the fanatical savages of the Pathet Lao. If that wasn't bad enough, their method of entrance into the operational area was bizarre and dangerous. This type of transport into battle hadn't been used in active combat in more than twenty years. It had even been labeled obsolete by the military experts. But this didn't deter the Black Eagles from the idea.

They used a glider to make a silent flight to a secret landing zone. If that wasn't bad enough, the operations plan called for their extraction through a glider-recovery apparatus that had never been tested in combat.

After a hairy ride in the flimsy craft, they hit the ground to carry out a mission designed to destroy the construction site of a Soviet nuclear power plant the

Reds wanted to install in the area. Everything went wrong from the start, and the Black Eagles fought against a horde of insane zealots until their extraction to safety. This was completely dependent on the illegal and unauthorized efforts of a dedicated U.S.A.F. pilot — the same man they had rescued from the North Vietnam prison camp. The Air Force colonel was determined to help the same men who had saved him, but many times even the deadliest determination isn't enough.

This hairy episode was followed with two occurrences: The first was Capt. Robert Falconi's promotion to major, and the second was a mission that had been doubly dangerous because of an impossibility to make firm operational plans. Unknown Caucasian personnel, posing as U.S. troops, had been committing atrocities against Vietnamese peasants. The situation had gotten far enough out of control that the effectiveness of American efforts in the area had been badly damaged. Once again Falconi and the Black Eagles were called upon to sort things out. They went in on a dark beach from the submarine and began a deadly reconnaissance until they finally made contact with their quarry. These enemy agents, wearing U.S. army uniforms, were dedicated East German Communists prepared to fight to the death for their cause. The Black Eagles admired such unselfish dedication to the extent that they gave the Reds the opportunity to accomplish that end — give their lives for Communism. But this wasn't accomplished without the situation deteriorating to the point the Black Eagles had to endure human wave assaults from a North Vietnamese Army battalion led by an infuriated general. This officer had been humiliated by Falconi on the Song Bo River several months previously. The mission

28

ended in another Black Eagle victory — but not before five more men had died.

Brought back to Saigon at last, the seven survivors of the previous operations had cleaned their weapons, drawn fresh, clean uniforms and prepared for a long-awaited period of R&R.

It was not to be.

Chuck Fagin's instincts and organization of agents had ferreted out information that showed a high-ranking intelligence officer of the South Vietnamese Army had been leaking information on the Black Eagles to his superiors up in the Communist north. It would have been easy enough to arrest this double agent, but an entire enemy espionage net had been involved. Thus, Falconi and his Black Eagles had to come in from the boondocks and fight the good fight against these spies and assassins in the back streets and alleys of Saigon itself.

When Saigon was relatively cleaned up, the Black Eagles drew a mission that involved going out on the Ho Chi Minh Trail on which the North Vietnamese sent supplies, weapons and munitions south to be used by the Viet Cong and elements of the North Vietnamese army. The enemy was enjoying great success despite repeated aerial attacks by the U.S. and South Vietnamese Air Forces. The high command decided that only a sustained campaign conducted on the ground would put a crimp in the Reds' operation.

Naturally, they chose the Black Eagles for the dirty job.

Falconi and his men waged partisan warfare in its most primitive and violent fashion with raids, ambushes, and other forms of jungle fighting. The order of the day was "kill or be killed" as the monsoon forest thundered with reports of numerous types of modern weaponry, while the more insidious and deadly form of mine warfare made each track and trail through the brush a potential zone of death.

When this was wrapped up, Falconi and his troops received an even bigger assignment. This next operation involved working with Chinese mercenaries to secure an entire province ablaze with infiltration and invasion by the North Vietnamese Army. This even involved beautiful Andrea Thuy, a lieutenant in the South Vietnamese Army who had been attached to the Black Eagles. Playing on the mercenaries' superstitions and religions, she became a "Warrior-Sister" leading some of the blazing combat herself.

An affair of honor followed this mission, when Red agents kidnapped this lovely woman. They took her north — but not for long. Falconi and the others pulled a parachute-borne attack and brought her out of the hellhole where her Communist tormentors had put her.

The ninth mission, pulled off with most of the detachment's veterans away on R&R involved a full-blown attack by North Vietnamese regulars into the II Corps area — all this while saddled with a pushy newspaper reporter.

By that time South Vietnam had rallied quite a number of allies to her side. Besides the United States, there was South Korea, Australia, New Zealand, the Philippines and Thailand. This situation upset the Communist side and they decided to counter it by openly having various Red countries send contingents of troops to bolster to NVA (North Vietnam Army) and the Viet Cong.

This resulted in a highly secret situation — ironically well known by both the American and Communist sides — which developed in the borderland between

Cambodia and South Vietnam. The Reds, in an effort to make their war against the Americans a truly international struggle, began an experimental operation involving volunteers from Algeria. These young Arab Communists, led by hardcore Red officers, were tested against U.S. troops. If they proved effective, other nationals would be brought in from behind the Iron Curtain to expand the insurgency against the Americans, South Vietnamese, and their allies.

Because of the possibility of failure, the Reds did not want to publicize these "volunteers" to the conflict unless the experiment proved a rousing success. The American brass also did not want the situation publicized under any circumstances. To do so would be to play into the world opinion manipulations of the Communists.

But the generals in Saigon wanted the situation neutralized as quickly as possible.

Thus, Falconi and the Black Eagles moved into the jungle to take on the Algerians led by fanatical Maj. Omar Ahmed. Ahmed, who rebelled against France in Algeria, had actually fought in the French army in Indo-China as an enemy of the very people he ended up serving. Captured before the Battle of Dien Bien Phu, he had been an easy and pliable subject to the Red brainwashers and interrogators. When he returned to his native Algeria after repatriation, he was a dedicated Communist ready to take on anything the free world could throw at him.

Falconi and his men, with their communication system destroyed by deceit, fought hard. But they were badly outnumbered and finally forced into a situation where their backs were literally pinned against the wall of a jungle cliff. But Archie Dobbs, injured on the infiltration jump and evacuated from the mission, not only returned, but arrived in a helicopter gunship that threw in the fire support necessary to turn the situation around.

The Communist experiment was swept away in the volleys of aerial fire and the final bayonet charge of the Black Eagles. The end result was a promotion to lieutenant colonel for Falconi while his senior noncoms also were given a boost up the army's career ladder. Only Archie Dobbs, who had gone AWOL from the hospital, was demoted.

But the detachment had suffered much more than the loss of Archie's chevrons. Of the forty-four men who had either been assigned or attached to the unit, thirty-three had paid the supreme sacrifice of death on the battlefield. That added up to a casualty rate of a bit more than seventy-five percent.

During all those times, as unit integrity and morale built up despite the staggering losses, the detachment decided they wanted an insignia all their own. This wasn't at all unusual for units in Vietnam. Local manufacturers, acting on decisions submitted to them by the troops involved, produced these emblems that were worn by the outfits while "in country." These adornments were strictly nonregulation and unauthorized for display outside of Vietnam.

Falconi's men came up with a unique beret badge manufactured as a cloth insignia. A larger version was used as a shoulder patch. The design consisted of a black eagle — naturally — with spread wings. Looking to its right, the big bird clutched a sword in one claw and a bolt of lightning in the other. Mounted on a khaki shield that was trimmed in black, the device was an accurate portrayal of its wearers: somber and deadly.

There was one more touch of their individuality

32

that they kept to themselves. It was a motto which not only worked as a damned good password in hairy situations, but it also described the Black Eagles' basic philosophy.

Those special words, in Latin, were:

CALCITRA CLUNIS—KICK ASS!

CHAPTER 3

Chuck Fagin's arrival at Nui Dep heralded a big change in the Black Eagle's activities in the camp. Since their last operation, they had been taking it relatively easy. Falconi kept their physical edge sharp with tough exercising in the early hours of the morning that included a run around the camp perimeter. He also gave them brain exercise by holding classes on weaponry, small unit tactics, and other basic military skills.

But that was stopped now. Fagin was not there for drill or fun-and-games. He was there to get them back into the real shooting war. That meant there was a mission briefing in the offing, therefore the need for security was extra important. This was particularly necessary because of the indigenous militia in the camp. Not all of them were completely trustworthy, and several were no doubt Viet Cong plants. If an impending operation was tipped off, the Reds were sure to know of it within a matter of hours.

Therefore, Falconi's men were isolated in the area immediately surrounding their bunker. The gate in the high barbed wire fence around the place was shut tight, and a guard from Major Riley's Special Forces detachment was present twenty-four hours a day. Only persons with essential duties were allowed in or out.

Each man was given exact information on his part of the upcoming mission. Malpractice McCorckel was supplied with everything he needed to know on the medical and sanitary aspects of the war zone. Ray Swift Elk pored over intelligence reports and enemy orders of battle while Chief Petty Officer Brewster checked out the assigned frequencies and call signs for the communications end of activities.

They, and the others, took this data from the operations plan, maps and other documents that Fagin supplied them. For nearly seventy-two hours they studied and re-hashed this knowledge in an operations order. Typewriters clacked while the Black Eagles caucused in groups of twos and threes to sort through the paperwork and produce their own method of how they wanted to accomplish the mission assigned to them. A few arguments developed. Archie Dobbs even took an angry swing at Blue Richards over a disagreement concerning the best routes to follow, but Falconi stepped in and smoothed things over. Sometimes he pulled the combatants apart with a smile, kidding them back to happier moods. Other occasions required a damned good old-fashioned ass-chewing, and the lieutenant colonel could do that too.

As Archie Dobbs said, "When the skipper gets done taking a bite out of your ass, you need a bushel of Kotex to stop up the wound."

But the work did progress efficiently and quickly despite the set-backs until each individual and small group announced that they had completed their assignments.

Falconi knew they were suffering from mental and nervous fatigue. So, before proceeding further, he sent them outside for their first breaths of fresh air in three days and two nights. They had the luxury of a few extra hours, so the colonel was able to delay the proceedings until the next morning. At that time, each particular specialist could take his particular role in the planned action and present it to his buddies. That way every man in the detachment knew not only his own job, but that of each of the others.

When Falconi came topside from the bunker, they turned to meet his gaze. Archie, always the most vociferous, grinned. "You look like a man who wants to get a show on the road, Skipper."

"You read me loud and clear, Archie," Lieutenant Colonel Falconi said. "Let's get our asses below. I want you to put the final touches on your individual portions of the briefing so that they're letter perfect. You're getting a few hours' break, so take advantage of it."

One-by-one they returned to the earthen confines of their home.

The first in was Sgt. Maj. Top Gordon, the senior noncommissioned officer of the Black Eagles. His position required wearing several hats. Beside being tasked with taking the operations plan and using it to form the basic operations order for the missions, he was also responsible for maintaining discipline and efficiency within the unit. A husky man, his jetblack hair was thinning perceptibly, looking even more sparse because of the strict GI haircut he wore.

Gordon's entrance into the Black Eagles had been less than satisfactory. After seventeen years spent in the cloistered world of the 82nd Airborne Division, he had brought in a spit-and-polish attitude that did not fit well with the diverse individuals in Falconi's command. Gordon's zeal to follow army regulations to the letter had cost him a marriage several years previously, but he hadn't let up a bit. To make things worse, he had taken the place of a popular detachment sergeant who was killed in action on the Song Bo River. This noncom, called "Top" by the men, was an old Special Forces man who knew how to handle the type of soldier who volunteered for unconventional units. Gordon's first day in his new assignment brought him into quick conflict with the Black Eagle personnel that soon got so far out of hand that Falconi began to seriously consider relieving the sergeant and seeing to his transfer to the 173rd Airborne Brigade over in Tay Ninh province.

But during Operation Laos Nightmare, Gordon's bravery under fire earned him the grudging respect of the lower ranking Black Eagles. Finally, when he fully realized the problems he had created for himself, he changed his methods of leadership. Gordon backed off doing things by the book and found he could still maintain good dicipline and efficiency while getting rid of the chicken-shit aspects of army life. It was most apparent he had been accepted by the men when they bestowed the nickname "Top" on him.

He had truly become the "top sergeant" then.

The next man in the bunker was Sgt. 1st Class Calvin Culpepper. This tall, brawny black man had entered the army from a poor Georgia farm his family worked as sharecroppers. He handled the explosives chores that popped up from time to time. His favorite tool was C4 plastic explosives, and Calvin was reputed to be able to put a shaped charge under a silver dollar, touch it off and get back ninety-nine cents in change. He was a virtuoso with the Claymore mine as well, and used it to its best advantage. Ten years of dedicated service in the United States Army had produced an excellent soldier. Resourceful, intelligent, and combatwise, Calvin pulled his weight — and then a bit more — in the dangerous undertakings of the Black Eagles.

The detachment medic, Sgt. 1st Class Malcomb McCorckel, came in on Calvin's heels. An inch under six feet in height, he was affectionately called "Malpractice" by the other Black Eagles. He would have preferred the more common nickname "Doc" as was used for most other medical corpsmen, but the appellation stuck. Malpractice had been in the Army for twelve years. He had a friendly face and spoke softly as he pursued his duties in seeing after the illnesses and hurts of his buddies. As nagging and worrisome as a mother hen, he took his responsibilities seriously enough to make himself a real pain in the ass — literally when it came to penicillin shots. The other guys bitched back at him, but not angrily, because each Black Eagle appreciated his concern. They all knew that nothing devised by puny man could keep Malpractice from reaching a wounded detachment member and pulling him back to safety.

Master Sgt. Ray Swift Elk was responsible for the unit's intelligence work. A full-blooded Sioux Indian from South Dakota, he was lean and muscular. His copper-colored skin, prominent nose, and high cheekbones gave him the appearance of the classic prairie warrior. And, indeed, he was a direct descendant of the braves who had held the United States Army at bay over a long period of years in the 19th century. Twelve years of service in Special Forces made him particularly well-qualified in his slot. Part

38

of his tribe's history included some vicious combats against the black troopers of the U.S. Cavalry's 9th and 10th Regiments of the racially segregated Army of the 1800s. The Sioux warriors had nicknamed the black men they fought "Buffalo Soldiers". This was because of their hair which, to the Indians, was like the thick manes on the buffalo. The cognomen was a sincere compliment due to these Native Americans' veneration of the bison. Ray Swift Elk called Calvin Culpepper "Buffalo Soljer", and he did it with the same respect his ancestors had used during the Plains Wars.

The man with the most perilous job in the detachment was Cpl. Archie Dobbs, and no other unit in the army had a man quite like him. A brawling, beer-swilling womanizer, Archie was a one-man public scandal and disaster area in garrison or in town. But out in the field, as point man and scout, he went into dangerous areas first, just to see what — or who — was there. Reputed to be the best compass man in the United States Army, his seven years of service was fraught with stints in the stockade and dozens of "busts" to lower rank. Fond of women and booze, Archie's claim to fame — and the object of genuine respect from the other men — was that he had saved their asses on more than one occasion by guiding them safely through throngs of enemy troops behind the lines. Like the cat who always landed on his feet, Archie could be dropped into the middle of any geographic hell and find his way out. His sense of direction was flawless, making him the Man-of-the-Hour on several Black Eagle missions during dangerous exfiltration operations when everything had gone completely and totally to shit.

Archie was followed into the bunker by PO Blue

Richards, a Navy Seal. He was a red-haired Alabaman with a gawky, good-natured grin common to good ol' country boys. Blue had been named after his "daddy's favorite huntin' dawg." An expert in demolitions either on land or under water—Blue considered himself honored for his father to have given him that dog's name.

The new man, Marine Staff Sgt. Paulo Garcia, came in on Blue's heels. A former tuna fisherman from San Diego, Garcia had joined the Marines at the relatively late age of twenty-one after deciding to look for a bit more adventure. There was plenty of Marine activity to see around his hometown, and he decided the Corps offered him exactly what he was looking for. Ten years of service, and plenty of combat action in the Demilitarized Zone and Khe Sanh made him more than qualified for the Black Eagles.

The unit's supply sergeant came in on Garcia's heels. He was a truly talented and enterprising staff sergeant named Enrique "Hank" Valverde, and had been in the army for ten years. He began his career as a supply clerk, quickly finding ways to cut through Army red tape to get logistical chores taken care of quickly and efficiently. He made the rank of sergeant in the very short time of only two years, finally volunteering for the Green Berets in the late 1950s. Hank Valverde found that Special Forces was the type of unit that offered him the finest opportunity to hone and practice his near legendary supply expertise.

Hank was followed into the bunker by U.S. Navy CPO Leland Brewster. Although born and bred in Iowa, he was a sea-going man at heart. The myriad of tattoos covering his arms and body attested to his devotion to being a real "sailorman." The only problem Chief Brewster had was that he always found more action ashore. So he volunteered for the Seals in order to enjoy the best of both worlds. With a seamed, leathery face and an easy smile, this veteran of fifteen years in the Navy brought diverse and long experience in communications into the Black Eagles with him. He was a natural choice to be Falconi's commo chief.

The final man to enter the bunker was the recently appointed second-in-command now with one Black Eagle mission under his belt. He was Lt. Chris Hawkins who, like Chief Brewster and Blue Richards, was a Navy Seal. A graduate of Annapolis, he had five years of service which included plenty of clandestine operations on the coast of North Vietnam. A tall, rangy but muscular New Englander, he was descended from seven generations of a family devoted to the sea as ship's owners, masters and navigators. Chris spent his youth sailing and swimming the waters off his native Massachusetts, which made him an even more natural sailor then Brewster. His service in the Seals combined that seamanship with tough soldiering skills, making him a natural for the Black Eagles.

Chuck Fagin, sitting with the chopper pilot Stensland and the gunner Gunnar Olson, was already sitting at Falconi's desk drinking a cup of lukewarm coffee. He had a love/hate relationship with the Black Eagles. Although they truly felt he did his very best for them, sometimes the unit believed he didn't fight hard enough when they were in certain difficult positions, such as being cut off behind enemy lines and surrounded.

Fagin didn't give a damn about winning any popularity contests. He'd done his own stint behind enemy lines as a member of the OSS in World War II. He'd lived in the hills with Yugoslavian guerrillas, isolated for more than a year while an elite anti-partisan *Waffen SS* battalion hunted for them. Fagin was dedicated to winning the wars he served in, whether as a soldier or a CIA operative directing military operations. While he regretted any man under his control dying, he was more than willing to accept losses.

Fagin stood up. "Before you get back to your work, I want to make an official statement regarding Mister Stensland and Specialist Olson. I realize that you all know they will be flying aerial fire support on this mission. You've all worked with Stensland on the last mission when he and Archie pulled off a very unauthorized sortie to lend a hand. When I found out we were being given gunship support, I personally chose him for his flying ability and guts. Stensland chose Olson for his gunner. That was good enough for me. I just want you guys to know you've got the best backing you up."

A round of applause broke out. Stensland made a mock bow, but Gunnar the Gunner Olson showed no emotion. His tough Scanadinavian face remained impassive. The pilot also acted as their spokesman. "We're both glad to be with the best," he flatly stated. "We'll be looking forward to seeing you later."

Stensland and Gunnar the Gunner would be leaving the next morning before the briefing. This was because the security was so tight. All information regarding the mission was on a strick need-to-know basis. Since the two airmen didn't really need to be concerned with movement or certain other aspects of the operation, their presence was not required.

Falconi went to his desk, then turned and glared at his men. "What the hell are you jokers standing around for?"

They immediately went back to their paperwork tasks and gave the project their full attention.

When the Falcon growls, the Black Eagles jump!

CHAPTER 4

Chuck Fagin, Erick Stensland, and Gunnar the Gunner Olson left early that next morning. Their departure was the same as their arrival, with the CIA operative going out on the regularly scheduled H34 and the Cobra gunship trailing behind through the blistering tropical sky.

The activity in the Black Eagles' bunker was somber and businesslike as the men gathered around for their mission briefing. The electric fans buzzed, sending cigarette smoke — and Top's cigar fumes — swirling through the still, hot atmosphere. Despite the heat, several men sipped after-breakfast hot coffee from their canteen cups. The meal hadn't been much, only C-rations, but the excitement of the upcoming operation had taken the edge off their appetites anyhow.

Lieutenant Colonel Falconi walked to the front of the room. The men instantly quieted down their conversations and gave him full attention. Falconi took a sip of his own coffee before he spoke:

"Here we go again."

There was a shuffling of chairs and bodies as the men instinctively leaned forward to hear better.

44

Falconi used his pointer to indicate a sector on the map of Vietnam mounted on the wall. "Communist patrol boats have infiltrated the Song Cai River and now control the waterway north of Dak Bla," he said beginning the situation portion of the briefing. "Their activities range from actual raiding of river villages and military outposts, to active operations involving the transportation and infiltration of Red agents."

Archie Dobbs, always interested in geography, squinted at the map. "Say, Skipper, ain't the Song Cai in South Vietnam?"

"Correct," Falconi answered. "But despite that fact, it is now under the complete control of the Viet Cong and elements of the North Vietnamese Army. They virtually own that river now."

The men had now located the exact area on their individual maps they'd folded out on their laps. Calvin Culpepper made a quick, but accurate map reconnaissance of the entire run of the Song Cai. He looked up at his commanding officer. "So what're they telling us to do, sir?"

"Our mission is simple," Falconi replied. "Get that river back."

"All of it?" Archie asked facetiously.

"Every goddamned drop in it," Falconi answered. "If there're no further questions about the situation or the mission assigned us, I'll turn the briefing over to Top for the execution portion."

The detachment's top sergeant took Falconi's place. He wasted no time in warming up to the task. "This afternoon at 1400 hours we will meet a C-130 air transport at the airstrip and board her for a flight to Chu Lai. After arriving at that destination, which is only a stop on the way, we'll board deuce-and-halfs for a convoy run to Dak Bla."

"Truck convoy?" Blue Richards moaned.

"That's right," Top said. "You'll be getting your asses bounced around pretty good too. It's estimated that the trip will take about eighteen hours — provided there are no ambushes by the VC on the way."

The new man, Paulo Garcia, was confused. "How come we're going by truck, Top? Can't we land at Dak Bla?"

"Ordinarily we would," Top explained. "But the amount of infiltration by the Charlies on the Song Cai has made that place a security nightmare. If we came in there directly, the Reds operating on the Song Cai would be aware of our presence within a few hours. And they would be ready for us too."

Ray Swift Elk, the perennial intelligence man, understood perfectly. "But if we came in on a regularly scheduled convoy, nobody would notice us in particular."

"Especially since there'll be other troops aboard those trucks too," Top said. "We'll simply be part of a milling throng for a while. After dark we'll head north for a rendezvous on the Song Cai at a point northeast of Dak Bla." He pointed to the exact position on the map. "It is then and there that we pick up our three boats."

"Boats?" Blue Richards beamed. "We're going aboard boats."

Top grinned at him. "That's right, sailor. You're gonna be a seaman again — or at least a riverman — how's that sound?"

"Great!" Blue exclaimed.

Chief Petty Officer Brewster wanted to know a bit more. "What kinda craft are they, Top?"

"Chris will cover that in his briefing," Top said. "But once we're aboard we'll move out to our main operating base which will be the village of Tam

Nuroc. From that point on we'll take appropriate action to do as we've been charged to do: get the fucking river back."

There was a brief moment of sullen silence. Their last mission had also been a "play-it-by-ear" situation, and they'd ended up surrounded and cut-off. Only Archie Dobbs's intervention with Erick Stensland's OH-6A gunship had pulled them out of that particular pile of shit.

Top, the ever-wise senior non-commissioned officer, sensed the mood. He grinned at them. "Hell, guys, we've always operated that way, haven't we?" He laughed. "Even if the brass gave us a play-by-play plan to follow, we'd still do it Falconi's way."

"And kick lots of ass too!" Calvin Culpepper added. The others indicated their agreement with some shouted laughter.

"Damn straight," Top said. "Any questions on the execution of the mission?"

"Am I right in assuming we'll stay on ops until we own that river again?" Archie Dobbs asked.

"That's right," Top said. "There was nothing about a time limit or relief in the operations plan that Fagin toted down to us." He waited for more questions. There were none. "Okay," Top said picking up his notes. "Ray Swift Elk will give us the intelligence portion of the briefing."

Master Sergeant Swift Elk, slim and imposing, strode up to the front of the room. Slightly bowlegged, he appeared as if he'd be more comfortable on the back of a horse. "The enemy we are to face is a specially trained river combat unit consisting of approximately six power boats," Swift Elk said.

"Six?" Malpractice asked. "And we'll have three, huh? That means we're outnumbered two to one."

"Yeah," Swift Elk said calmly. "But what the hell?

47

On the last mission against the camel-jockeys, they had us about a hundred to thirteen. My fingers and toes figgered that out to be odds o' more than seven to one."

"And we damned near got creamed," Malpractice complained. "Kim, Bernstein and Taylor bought the farm."

"Bring some extry bandages," Blue Richards laughed.

Malpractice smiled wryly. "I always do, pal."

"Okay, let's get on with this," Swift Elk said. "Like I said, they have six boats. They're Chinese Communist motor torpedo boats that have been modified for river work. The torpedo tubes have been taken out—"

"Thank God for small favors," Chief Brewster interrupted.

"—but they are heavily armed with machine guns and rocket launchers," Swift Elk continued. "Each carries a section of soldiers and a crew of about ten men." He glanced at Malpractice. "So it's sixty to—" Swift Elk paused and counted the guys in the room. "—sixty to eleven."

"Oh, goody!" Archie Dobbs exclaimed. "That means I can shoot five or six of 'em and go home."

Malpractice frowned. "You guys give me a pain. I got to nurse you through all your hurts, and you go into this shit like ever'thing is gonna be all right. Well, I ain't no miracle worker."

"Hell, we ain't worried, Malpractice," Archie said. "We know you're the best damned medic in the Army."

"I have to be," Malpractice retorted. "If I wasn't, all you crazy fuckers would be dead or in the hospital."

"Hey!" Ray Swift Elk yelled. "Do you guys mind? I am delivering a briefing here."

48

"At ease!" Top roared in his best 82nd Airborne Division style. Then he added, "Shut the fuck up."

"Okay," Swift Elk went on. "The river is a muddy sumbitch. It's the kind they describe in South Dakota as too thin to plow and too thick to drink. The land around it is heavily overgrown jungle. It's deadly, guys, and we'll be facing ambushes all the way up and down that waterway. So let's be extra alert. And keep your yaps closed while we're at Tam Nuroc or any of the other settlements and villages. You can be damned sure that those places will be crawling with VC agents, and they'd like nothing better than to tip their buddies about what we'll be up to. Security has a top priority. If you gotta talk about the ops, keep your voices down and only do it when absolutely necessary."

Calvin Culpepper looked over at Archie Dobbs and winked. "You must really be in love with that li'l nurse of yours, Archie."

"Why do you say that?" Archie asked puzzled.

"Hell! You didn't ask nothing about the women in them little towns," Calvin said.

They all laughed, but it was Malpractice McCorckel who broached the question. "What about those women?"

"You'll get pussy there if you want it," Swift Elk said. "You might have to buy it, but there's females available."

"Hey, Malpractice!" Blue Richards yelled. "How come *you're* so damn curious about the womenfolk? You lookin' for romance, boy?"

"No way!" Malpractice said. "I just wanted to know if I have to bring along some extra penicillin to treat you idiots for the clap."

Falconi interrupted the laughter that followed. "Let's go, guys. We have a briefing to finish here."

49

"I have nothing more," Swift Elk said. "So I'll turn you over to Hank Valverde for the poop on supply."

Hank Valverde was the hardest working member of the detachment. The logistics of a specialized unit like the Black Eagles required endless hours and was a paperwork nightmare. Hank not only had to work with numerous Army supply echelons and depots, but on other occasions he had to cross service lines and deal with the Air Force and Navy.

His face was sullen as he faced the unit. "I have an announcement regarding weapons. Even though it's still okay for you guys to carry in personal weapons, our issue has been changed due to an administrative quirk. SOG's S4 no longer is concerned with ordnance. We've been put into the regular mill for that. The result is that the only stuff we'll be carrying will be M16s. No mortars, no machine guns, no M79 grenade launchers—just the M16s."

"No goddamned M79s!" Calvin Culpepper cursed. "What're we gonna do? Toss hand grenades now?"

"You'll be carrying grenades all right," Hank said. "But for the longer ranges, we'll have our grenadiers rely on attaching M203s to their M16s."

There were some collective moans from the group.

"But there's a brighter side to this," Hank assured them. "I know we've all grown fond and accustomed to the M79s, but the M203s are handier because everything is contained in one weapon. I was a grenadier on the last operation, and I can tell you it got to be a real pain switching from an M16 to the M79 ever'time I wanted to fire a grenade. Particularly while I was doing it on the run."

Paulo Garcia spoke up. "He's right, guys. I've used 'em both and, believe me, the M203 is better. It's got some nasty ammo to go with it too. There's even a bouncing round that hits the ground, and a small charge sends it five feet up into the air before it explodes."

"Air burst!" Blue Richards exclaimed.

"You got it!" Paulo said.

"So let's cheer up, guys," Hank said. "Now to get to the other goodies. We'll be getting fuel and other supplies at Tam Nuroc. The skipper will estimate the various lengths of times we'll be out on the river, and we'll draw the predetermined amounts of items as needed. There'll be no aerial supplies to have to rely on this time. We'll have C-rations for chow, plus whatever goodies we can get off the locals. There is also abundant fishing, so we at least won't get hungry."

"Don't stuff yourselves!" Malpractice warned them. "You'll get indigestion and belly wounds are doubly dangerous after you've been eating."

"Thank you, Mother Hubbard!" Archie smirked.

Valverde made another silent check of items on the paper attached to his clipboard. "Okay. That's it from your friendly supply sergeant. I'll let Chief Brewster take over now with the communications poop."

The heavily tattooed Navy man stepped to the front as Hank left to tend to some demanding logistics chore. The chief folded his muscular arms. "There ain't much to tell you swabs," he said. "The commo on this here trip is gonna be light and easy. All they're giving us is PRC-6s, so they ain't expecting us to do any fancy communicating at any great distance between ourselves. But we will have an AN/PRC-41 to talk to Eric Stensland's chopper and the rear base. That particular call sign is 'Abner'. We'll call Erick and Gunnar the Gunner 'Norski' over the air. The skipper will handle that hisself."

Chris Hawkins was concerned. "Any idea who 'Abner' is, Chief?"

The chief shook his head. "I know who it ain't, Mister Hawkins. It ain't Chuck Fagin. Anyhow, the upshot of it all is, the commo will be on the KISS principle—Keep It Simple, Stupid." He grinned. "Looks like there won't be much for me to do but tote a rifle and be a grunt like you other guys."

"Welcome to the club," Archie Dobbs said.

"Glad to be aboard," the chief said. "I ain't got much more to talk about, so I'll leave the floor to Malpractice."

The medic came forward. He wasted no time in launching into one of his tirades. "Don't drink that fucking dirty river water. People wash in it, piss in it and shit in it. The only thing that ain't been dumped into the Song Cai its factory waste, and that's only because this ain't a developed industrial nation. We'll be taking potable water with us. If you get into a desperate situation, then use them purification tablets I keep throwing at you guys. I'll be passing out salt tablets too. You'll take 'em or else."

"Or else what?" Archie asked playfully.

Malpractice frowned. "Or I'll kick your ass so far up between your ears you'll have to fart through your nose."

"Okay! Okay!" Archie exclaimed. "Christ! You're such a grouch sometimes!"

"And if you Romeos got the urge to poke any of them women, use a goddamned rubber and come to me for a pro treatment," Malpractice said. "You can be sure that any broad that'd let one of you ugly ducklings have a go at her would be willing to bed down a syphilitic water buffalo. So just figger she's infected, and act accordingly."

"You ain't talking to me, man," Archie countered, thinking of Betty Lou Pemberton. "I got a nice girl."

"Wonderful," Malpractice said insincerely. "Now

watch scratches, insect bites, bruises and the like. You all know how easy it is to get infections out in the jungle, especially around a dirty river. Do what I say. Now I'll turn this over to Chris."

Chris Hawkins was smiling widely when he went to the front of the detachment. "I guess you know that there's three real happy Navy men now that we're going aboard boats."

"What kind are they giving us, Mister Hawkins?" Chief Brewster asked.

"Ones you're real familiar with," Chris answered. "They're LCPL Mark IIs."

The chief laughed. "For you lubbers, that means we'll be going aboard Landing Craft, Personnel, Launch."

"Right," Chris said. "These are modified for our use. They're powered by 300 horsepower Gray marine diesel engines that can get the craft up to some 17 knots of speed. Running with a river current should be even better. They're thirty-six feet long and we should get about 17-plus nautical miles on a tankful of gas."

"Again for the lubbers," the chief said. "That's more'n nineteen regular miles."

"But we'll be carrying extra gasoline," Chris added.

"That'll make us floating bombs," Top Gordon remarked.

Falconi used one of his favorite expressions. "Nobody said this job was going to be easy."

"Amen!" Calvin Culpepper added.

"We'll have a few hours to train on the craft before we take them to war," Chris said. "So a few of you will be expert yachtsmen before this is over." He looked over at Falconi. "The floor is yours, sir."

"Thanks, Chris." Falconi went to the front. "There're plenty of lessons for us to learn. River navigation, powerboating and amphibious warfare are going to be added to our basic skills of jungle fighting. We've got a real plus in airship gun support from Erick Stensland and his pal Gunnar the Gunner in their chopper."

"The Naughty Norski," Archie said reminding them all of the name given the helicopter by her intrepid crew.

"Right," Falconi said. "But despite the Naughty Norski, we're outnumbered and outgunned, so we'll just wade in over our heads and follow the unit motto — *Calcitra Clunis* — kick ass!" He turned to the Top. "Sergeant Major, take over the detachment."

Top didn't make a ceremony out of it. "Go get packed. And hurry up about it. You want to live forever?"

CHAPTER 5

Madame Fleurette Hue sat in her simple, rustic office and sipped the early evening cup of tea that had become a ritual with her over the years. As a person who did most of her work during the hours of darkness, she found the extra push of caffeine helpful in fighting the drowsiness she had never been able to overcome during the late nights of the oldest profession.

The lady looked through the wide window screen at the thick jungle only scant meters away. She paid a rice farmer's adolescent son to maintain a daily machete assault on the stubborn vegetation's growth to keep it away from her thatch-roofed building.

Madame Hue was an attractive woman, her almond eyes lively and sensual, and there was a dainty aura about her which gave a hint of tea ceremonies and food served in fragile china dishes. Actually she ran a whorehouse on the Song Cai River.

The place wasn't fancy, but its bamboo walls and thatch roof were strongly constructed and offered the maximum of privacy to the customers. A large sitting room, complete with western furniture, occupied a large portion of the front. A dozen cribs, each with narrow bed, a stand complete with basin and pitcher, one chair and a shelf boasting wire hangers, occupied the greatest percentage of the building. Fleurette's office, quite small and modest, was set in the back. Here she kept her books and dealt with other administrative details of the enterprise.

Now in her mid-forties, Fleurette was no newcomer to prostitution. She had been in the business since the age of ten. Her father, a poor inland peasant, had sold the girl to a Chinese whorebroker who traveled among the poverty-stricken villages in the lower mountains. He made a small fortune locating beautiful and comely children of both sexes. After either personally finding one, or having his agents perform the task, he would begin direct and honest bargaining with the father, offering hard cash for the child he was interested in. Most peasant families had plenty of kids but lacked many material things beyond the rice they harvested and the handwoven clothes on their backs. The chance for some real money was too much of a temptation for many a man, and he would let one of his many children go for a few thousand piasters. Of course, if he realized his son or daughter had special qualities, he could be stubborn enough to get even gold or silver after some hard-nosed bargaining.

This had been the case for Fleurette. Her father had gotten plenty from the merchant. Since he already had four other daughters, the peasant felt no particular loss. But Fleurette had cried and wailed when the Chinese merchant took her away. Despite her behavior, she was well-treated during the journey down to Hanoi. This wasn't so much out of kindness, as for commercial reasons. A well-fed, healthy child brought more cash than a miserable one covered by bruises and welts. There was little Fleurette could do in any case, and she soon accepted her fate with the usual Oriental stoicism.

Fleurette Hue had, indeed, been a beautiful child. After the good price she'd fetched for her father, she brought a handsome profit to her Chinese master—almost a thousand per cent increase in his investment for the wily old sonofabitch—and the girl was placed in an elegant brothel in Hanoi.

Here, under the tutelage of the madame and designated older prostitutes, Fleurette was initiated early into the world of sex. Her first actual experience was with a boy not much older than her. Although he served male homosexuals, he was a heterosexual himself and preferred female partners to male ones. Because of this, he was chosen to gently take the girl-child through a series of lessons not much different than what teenagers in western nations experienced. They started with handholding, gentle kisses and caresses, then went through heavier and heavier petting until they were indulging in regular bouts of sexual intercourse.

After that Fleurette's schooling went into the more exotic aspects of oral and anal sex until she was ready for the big time—real customers. There would be wealthy Oriental businessmen with particular erotic desires to be satisfied. And it was all done elegantly and with some degree of formality and, surprisingly, even dignity.

Fleurette Hue stayed in that same bordello until her early twenties. By then she was a beautiful woman with a well-established clientele of wealthy men who gave her more than the going price. She received jewelry, clothing, furniture and even stocks and bonds in some cases. The end result was that the shrewd and thrifty lady of the evening was able to buy out her own contract and go into business for herself.

She set herself up in a luxury apartment in one of Hanoi's finest suburbs, and expanded her list of customers to include French army officers. Fleurette's popularity among these young men brought her to the attention of the senior colonels and generals, and by the time the French Indo-Chinese War was in full swing, she had an impressive group of men calling on her for sexual favors. These customers were the ones who actually gave her the name Fleurette—Little Flower—now included high-ranking bureaucrats and other government officials.

After a couple of years practicing her lucrative profession, Fleurette attracted attention from another quarter—the Communist Viet Minh.

These Red agents had no interest in her for their own personal sexual desires. They had singled her out as an excellent source of intelligence. Her numerous customers, many times drunk, were sure to babble at least one or two state and military secrets during the course of a given week. All the Communists wanted of Fleurette was to take notes and remember what was said. Then, of course, she was to report it to them in full and complete detail.

Fleurette at first refused. She recognized that she needed a close rapport of trust and confidence with her customers. The young whore did not want to jeopardize her standing with the clients. But the local Viet Minh agent pointed out to her, quite realistically, that she would have trouble entertaining such high-class men if her face was worked over with a straight razor.

Fleurette, at the mercy of the authorities anyhow, saw that resistance was useless. She gave in and did as they asked. From the years 1950 to 1954 she supplied the Reds with invaluable information regarding all phases of French military and civil actions in their war against the Communist insurgency. The intelligence she gleaned was instrumental in several heavy French defeats.

When the armistice was finally signed that created North and South Vietnam, the Communists ordered her to give up her Hanoi operation and move south. They even supplied her with money to set up her own whorehouse in Saigon. Now, instead of servicing customers herself, she oversaw the activities of other women.

Fleurette hired some local talent, and did quite well in her new business until the arrival of the Americans. The local crime syndicate took over all prostitution and brought it under their control. The new set-up cut down the number of actual operations. Since Fleurette was not an original Saigon madame, she was told to leave the city and take her establishment elsewhere. Naturally, the young woman turned to her Red supporters for help, but they were unable to give her any assistance. Taking on the local gangsters would cause a big ruckus that would draw attention to the Viet Cong cells operating in the capital.

Fleurette Hue's fortunes took a bad nose-dive. She was finally forced to open up a small operation north of Dak Bla on the Song Cai River. The money wasn't good most of the time, but there were troops traveling through the area. When a unit arrived, her girls really went to work. The soldiers lined up outside while Fleurette took their money. One after another they went to the first available stall, took the whore, then left by the back door. Very inelegant for a woman who had once entertained French generals and diplomats.

But there was one thing that didn't change in

Fleurette's life: the Communists still kept a hold on her—like it or not.

The C-130 troop carrier landed heavily on the runway at Chu Lai. As the aircraft taxied toward the unloading point, the Black Eagles inside unbuckled their seat belts and began to gather up their gear.

They were dressed in generic uniforms—including steel helmets—and from outward appearances could pass for a regular infantry detachment instead of a team of specialized military experts. A casual observer might even guess they were a quartermaster or transportation group arriving for assignment to one of the truck companies stationed in the area.

The engines were cut, and the crew chief opened the door. He lowered the ladder and stepped back. Although he didn't know exactly who these passengers were, he had rightly surmised they were a special group, particularly since they'd gotten on the plane at a remote Special Forces B Camp. He knew damned well these weren't truck drivers or blanket-counters.

"Good luck, guys," he said. "See you on another trip sometime."

"You bet," Lieutenant Colonel Falconi said. He wore no insignia of rank, and enjoyed being informal with the sergeant. It was people like the Air Force man that kept things humming with transportation, food, ammo and all the other essentials the fighting men needed to carry on their own deadly jobs.

Falconi stepped onto the concrete, then waited for Top Gordon to follow. The newly promoted sergeant major went to extra trouble to form the men up properly. The Black Eagles normally didn't perform close-order drill—and were damned poor at it when they did, since they were out of practice—but they would have to march around a bit in order to create the impression they were regular troops.

"Form up!" Top barked. He suppressed a laugh and kidded Archie as the scout left the aircraft. "Hey, soldier. What'd you shine them boots with? A Hershey bar?"

Archie winked at him. "Hershey, hell! I used a Milky Way."

The others bumped and pushed each other as they fell into two ranks. Falconi glared at them. "Smarten up!" he whispered hoarsely. "The people watching us are supposed to figure we're fresh from the World."

The detachment did their best, but Top knew they looked like hell. "Dress right, dress!" he ordered in hopes of lining them up a little better. "Right, *face*! For'd, *march*!"

It was hopeless. An Air Force mechanic working on a nearby C-123 laughed out loud. "Ever'one o' them dudes got two left feet!" he guffawed.

The detachment also snickered among themselves, but finally managed to pick up the cadence as Top counted it off for them.

"Hup, two, t'ree, foh! Hup, two, t'ree, foh! Your left, your left, your left, right, left!"

Falconi noticed that the Marine Paulo Garcia looked sharp enough to please even the most discriminating drill instructor. "Garcia!" he said under his breath. "Take right guide."

Garcia broke formation and ran to the front of the right file to set the pace. He followed Top's count, and soon the others settled into the measured pace. By the time they arrived at the motor pool across the base, the Black Eagles weren't looking too bad.

The foreman of a Vietnamese civilian working crew looked up from supervising the gassing of the army trucks that his men were tending to. He waved at the detachment as they broke ranks and fell out to wait for further instructions.

"Hi, GIs! You new to 'Nam, hey?"

Blue Richards started to make a wisecrack in Vietnamese, but caught himself just in time. "Yeah," he said. "Where's them good looking women?"

"They all in town, pal," the foreman said. "You want a good time in Chu Lai, you ask for me. I am Happy Jack, best pal to GI American soljer. You bet!"

"I'll remember that," Blue said.

"You bet! You bet!" Happy Jack left them to inspect both his men and the vehicles. He checked the windshields for cleanliness, the air brake valves, then opened each cab for a look at the interior. At one vehicle, he climbed inside for a closer inspection, then dropped back down to the ground. "Okay! Okay! Squared away vehicles!" he called out in military terminology that was garbled by his accent. "You bet! You bet!"

A fat transportation master sergeant came out of the nearby motor pool shack. "We all set, Happy Jack?"

"You bet! Go for ride now. Plenty ready. You bet!"

Falconi stepped forward and handed a set of mimeographed orders to the sergeant. "We're detailed for this convoy."

"Sure pal," the sergeant said. "You guys are the first here, so you can pick whichever truck you want."

Falconi grinned. "We'll take the olive-drab one."

The sergeant laughed. "Hey, that's funny, pal." He suddenly became serious. "If I was you I'd avoid the front and the end of the convoy. Them's the poor bastards that get a pasting in an ambush."

"Gee!" Falconi said opening his eyes wide. "You think we might get shot at?"

The sergeant winked. "Who knows, pal? There's a war on, y'know. It ain't much of one, but like the old saying goes, 'It's the only one we got'."

Falconi counted the trucks. "There's nine of 'em," he said. "We'll take the fifth one. Okay?"

"Sure, pal. You're real smart. Go ahead and get on board. The supply stuff is already loaded on the others, and there's a few troops that'll be showing up with the drivers in another fifteen or twenty minutes."

"Gee, thanks," Falconi said. He motioned to the detachment. "You heard this here veteran. Let's get on that middle truck."

"Oh, boy!" Archie Dobbs said.

Fleurette heard the approaching boats long before they reached the dock in front of her bordello. She knew who it was even before her maid knocked on the door. "Captain Ngy and his men are arriving."

"Thank you," Fleurette said. "Make a fresh pot of tea, please."

"Yes, Madame."

Fleurette sat patiently for the time it took the three boats to tie up. It was only a matter of a few minutes after the engines were cut that there was a knock on her door.

"*Moi ong vao*," she invited.

The door opened and a North Vietnamese army officer entered. He took off his cap and affected a slight bow. "*Chao ba*," he greeted her.

"*Chao ong*. Please sit down. Would you care for tea?"

"Yes, thank you."

"How have you been, Captain Ngy?"

"Very busy, Madame Hue," he said. Their relationship was strictly businesslike and formal despite the fact that his men, even at that moment, were exchanging some of their cash for sexual favors with her girls.

The maid entered, and the two were quiet as the girl served them tea. When she had finished, she bowed deeply then retreated from the office.

Fleurette poured them both some of the hot brew. "I have some information. But none of it is particularly noteworthy. *Toi Tiec*."

The Communist officer sipped his tea. "Sometimes when a bit of intelligence seems useless, it later proves invaluable."

Fleurette handed him a piece of paper. "Some troop movements up and down the river by South Vietnamese river units. They do not go far."

"Of course not," Ngy said with a slight smile. "The river is ours." He set the cup down. "But, without a doubt, there will be an attempt to wrest it from us. When this happens, you will note newer, different troops. Perhaps military boats you've not seen before. If you warn us in time, we will be able to destroy the interlopers."

"Do not worry, Captain Ngy," Fleurette said. "You can rely on my girls and me to keep you fully informed."

Ngy picked up his cup again. This time he raised it in a toast. "To the People's Struggle."

"To the People's Victory," Fleurette added. She slowly sipped her tea while the captain studied the papers she had handed over to him.

Happy Jack waved at the convoy as it pulled away from the air base. Then, becoming all business, he directed his crew of workers to a group of trucks that needed washing. He set them to work, then left them to inspect another part of the motor pool where other vehicles awaited their attention. When he was sure no one was looking, he eased over to a place in the fence. The Vietnamese pulled a folded document from his jacket. He'd found it in the cab of the truck he'd crawled into.

There was a special opening in the fence, cleverly disguised, but Happy Jack knew exactly where it was. He slipped the document through the opening, then rearranged it again. There were others who would pick up the paper, and make good use of it.

It was a detailed route map of the convoy that had just left Chu Lai.

Happy Jack went back to supervise his workmen.

CHAPTER 6

The long, wooden bench-seats in the back of the two-and-a-half ton truck were hard and unforgiving. Never designed for paying passengers, the seats were put into the vehicle without the slightest consideration for luxurious travel.

The highway, actually a partially macadamed two-lane road that was bumpy and uneven, did nothing to lessen the discomfort of the long ride. Each pothole and dip rattled the truck frame, making the passengers bump into each other.

The physical side of the ride didn't bother the Black Eagles all that much. These were guys that could endure hunger, thirst, cold, heat and other hardships without griping too much. The type of men who would voluntarily throw themselves into ranger, parachute, Marine and SEAL training would scarcely notice a bumpy truck ride.

It was the psychological side of the situation that bugged them.

The Black Eagles were used to being on their own.

Once they had leaped from an airplane and left their parachutes upon landing, they did not generally have to depend on anybody to any great extent except for occasional resupply drops. But here in the back of a deuce-and-a-half they were at the mercy of not only a young driver who literally ran the machine, but they were shooting-gallery type targets to any crazy Viet Cong who might hide himself in the brush alongside the road waiting to rake the passengers helplessly stacked in the open area of the vehicle.

Their uneasiness was plain to see in the way they held their weapons and kept the muzzles trained on potential ambush sites that swept past their view.

Archie summed up the situation in his usual outspoken style: "Ain't this a bunch o' shit?"

Blue Richards licked his dry lips. "I feel like a damn ol' duck flyin' over Poacher's Pond."

Malpractice glanced at him. "Poacher's Pond?"

"Yeah," Blue said. "That's where my pappy hunts, and they ain't no duck gonna come flappin' over there without gittin' the feathers blowed off his ass by Pa."

Calvin Culpepper grinned. "I wish we had about a million rounds o' ammo. We could sit on both sides o' this truck and blast the surrounding country all the way up the road between Chu Lai and Dak Bla."

"No way, Buffalo Soljer," Ray Swift Elk said. "We'd burn out all the M16 barrels."

"Then we could fire them grenade launching M203s," Calvin said.

Hank Valverde disagreed with him on that one. "We couldn't tote that many grenades."

Calvin was undeterred. "Then, by God, we'd throw frigging rocks."

Chief Brewster looked up and laughed. "You're

67

forgetting how tired our arms would get."

"Okay then," Calvin offered. "How about *cussing* them sumbitches to death?"

Before any more wisecracks could be offered, there was a tremendous explosion at the head of the convoy. All eyes snapped forward at the exact moment to see a three-quarter ton truck rise in the air amidst a spewing plume of smoke, then somersault lazily back to the ground.

At the same time, their driver slammed on the brakes so hard they locked. The big truck spun around twice before slamming into the vehicle in front of it. The kid's head slammed into the windshield, but he scarcely noticed it. He stood up in the cab, blood streaming down his face from a deep gash. "Ambush!" he screamed. "Ambush! Ambush!"

"Hey, no shit?" Archie scowled. "I thought we was pulling into a drive-in movie. Get down, you dumb shit!"

The driver started to holler again, but was hit by automatic weapons fire. He jerked like a rag doll in a child's hands, then fell over the door to the road.

Falconi's M16 spewed out on full-auto. "Alpha left! Bravo right!"

Chris Hawkins led his Alpha Fire Team over the left side of the truck. Incoming small arms fire zinged around their heads and bounced off the metal portions of the truck. The team opened up immediately on their direct front, charging into the vegetation.

Top Gordon led the Bravos into a similar action on the right side. Paulo Garcia, more familiar with the M203 than anyone else in the detachment, had already inserted a buckshot M576 cannister into the weapon. He kicked off the round and blew away the nearby vegetation to his direct front. Two Viet Cong who had been hidden from view in the brush, were caught by the numerous steel pellets. The blast ripped them to bloody shreds. Their mangled bodies were swept a half dozen meters farther into the jungle.

Malpractice, as the team's automatic rifleman, swept the target area with well-controlled bursts of six and seven rounds while Top and Blue Richards pumped in individual shots to add to the Bravos' volleys.

Since most of the incoming fire was from the left, Falconi led the command element in that direction to join the Alphas. Their combined advance faltered after ten meters.

A Viet Cong heavy machine gun crew, the two men manning a Red Chinese Type 53, were damned good at their job. They had situated themselves back far enough to be able to cover a large portion of the ambush area. The 7.62-millimeter rounds were slicing through the vegetation about a meter off the ground.

Falconi and company hugged the dirt and cursed.

Swift Elk's M16 sprayed a couple of salvos, but all he did was attract their attention. He rolled away while dirt and leaves splattered around him in the hell of the machine gun fire.

Chris Hawkins turned his face over to one side and yelled at Calvin. "Try that launcher, Calvin!"

"No can do!" Calvin yelled back. "There's too damn many tree branches for it to hit."

Hawkins realized his grenadier was right. Any projectile fired would be more dangerous to the Black Eagles than to the enemy machine gun crew.

Falconi also had summed up the problem. He looked over at Archie who was situated handily on the extreme right flank. "What do you think?"

Archie pulled a handgrenade off his harness. "This looks like a hand job."

Hank Valverde leered at him. "Always thinking of sex, huh?"

"Yeah," Archie said crawling away. "I'm gonna give those fuckers the kiss o' death." He slithered into the brush.

"Open up on 'em!" Falconi ordered the rest of his men on that side of the battle.

The colonel, Chief Brewster and four Alphas gave everything they had for a full two minutes. Both Falconi and Swift Elk had their selectors on full auto. They swept back and forth while the others pumped in rapidly spaced shots.

Meanwhile Archie did a low crawl to reach the position he was looking for. His incredible ability to stay oriented despite distracting sounds, poor visibility and unfamiliar terrain, came to the fore.

The only problem was the two Viet Cong riflemen who were positioned in the middle of his intended route to the machine gun.

Archie's first reaction was to sneak around them, but he immediately ruled that out as a bad idea. Not only would it take more time, but there was a good probability that there were other VC he would run into anyway. He crawled quietly to a better firing position, then waited for the heavy machine gun to chug-a-chug out a few more rounds. When it did, he used the noise to cover the sound of his own weapon.

The first bullet hit the nearest VC in the temple. Brains and gore splattered out all over his buddy. The unhurt man, horrified by the mess on him, panicked and jumped up, brushing at the slimy stuff all over him.

Archie shot him once in the chest.

The Red fell with a twisting body, rolling over and sitting up in shock. The next round punched into his face and finished the job.

Archie rapidly but silently crawled between the two corpses and continued on his way. He kept a mental note of the sound from the heavy machine gun, and when he figured he'd gone between five and ten meters past it, the Black Eagle's detachment scout turned in.

He knew he'd done a good job of locating them when he noticed the lower leaves of some trees shaking from the big weapon's concussion each time it was fired. Archie got behind a tree and slowly stood up. He could see a couple of pith helmets, and knew he had the crew right where he wanted them. He pulled the grenade from his harness and wrested the pin out. After letting the spoon flip loose, he counted off to five and gave the explosive device a careful underhand toss.

It went over the bushes in a gentle lob and landed behind the crew. After bouncing once, it rolled between them. The two gunners had a millisecond of horror as their minds conceived what had rolled in their midst.

The grenade exploded, doing horrible damage at that close range. Archie followed this up with several quick firebursts at the gun position, then he wisely went to the ground.

Incoming rounds crashed a couple of feet above his head. These were from the Black Eagles who had immediately swept forward at the sound of the grenade's detonation. There were a couple of screams,

71

then several men rushed by Archie's position, and crashed into the jungle beyond.

"They're all gone!" Archie yelled at the top of his voice.

"Okay, Arch!" Falconi hollered back. "C'mon out!"

The scout stood up and walked back toward the road. There was a flurry of firing on the other side of the trucks showing that Top Gordon's Bravo Team was still engaged.

Archie joined the command element and the Alphas. "Let's go give Top and his guys a hand," he urged them.

Falconi, a couple of beats ahead of him, had already reversed their skirmish line. "Move out!"

Archie hurried forward to join his buddies as they hit the highway and rushed between the trucks to plunge into the battle that was raging between the Bravos and a stubborn group of Viet Cong who were damned good and pissed off about their ambush situation slipping out of their control.

The first two men they reached were Top and Paulo Garcia. The sergeant major signaled to Falconi and the lieutenant colonel joined him.

"We're pinned down," Top said. "We can move back without any real strain, but any frontal or flanking movements catch billy-be-damned hell!"

"Right," Falconi said appreciating the quick report. "We'll roll over on the right side."

Top knew what to do. "Open up on full-auto, everybody!" he yelled at his men. He looked at the Marine grenadier. "Paulo, throw out some more of that buckshot."

"You got it, Sergeant Major."

The Bravo's front exploded in a fury of increased firing. At the same time Falconi took his command element and the Alpha Fire Team in a direction perpendicular with the main battle line.

Then they made a hard left flank and charged into the farthest side of the enemy position. Viet Cong resistance melted away under the fusillades, and several of them went down under the steel hail.

"Once more, guys!" Falconi ordered.

They swung left again. This time they literally rolled up the enemy line while Top brought his own guys in from the front to bring the combat to an explosive, but quick finish.

Ray Swift Elk then went to work. "Buffalo Soljer! Blue!" he ordered. "Give me a hand searching the enemy dead."

In the meantime, Malpractice McCorckel had assured himself there were no Black Eagle casualties. "I'll see to the VC wounded," he said. "If there are any."

"I doubt it," Falconi remarked lighting a cigarette. "We put out enough fire power to blow away half the frigging Russian army."

Five minutes later Swift Eagle was examining some blood-soaked papers to see if there was anything of any intelligence value. He tossed them aside. "Nothing here, Skipper," he said to Falconi. "Only a couple of training schedules. No maps, rosters or orders."

Malpractice returned to the group. "You were right, Skipper. We didn't leave nothing but dead hunks of meat out there."

"Okay then, guys," Falconi ordered. "Back to the trucks."

The convoy, under the command of the experienced transportation sergeant, was already reorganized and ready to roll again. It was obvious he'd been ambushed before. The portly NCO didn't hide his curiosity when the Black Eagles rejoined the group. "Hey," he asked Falconi. "Who the hell are you guys anyhow?"

Archie answered the question. "I'll tell you who we ain't—the fucking Peace Corps."

"You can say that again," the sergeant said. "Them bastards knew what they was doing. When they blew up that first vehicle it blocked the road and made us stop." He shook his head. "If it wasn't for you guys, we'd been goners for sure."

Archie felt a little sorry for his flippant attitude. He now realized the guy put his life on the line every time he drove down that road. "Hey, Sarge. We're glad we could help. You transportation people are doing a damned good job keeping us in bullets and chow."

The sergeant looked at his three dead drivers laid out alongside the road. "Yeah," he said. "We're just *dying* to make a go of things around here."

"When we get to Dak Bla I want your name and unit," Falconi said. "You've got a letter of commendation coming."

"I don't know who you are," the sergeant said sensing these men were some sort of special elite unit, "but any appreciation is well received. But only if you put all my guys' names on that letter." He pointed to the young dead men. "Especially them. Okay?"

"Okay," Falconi said.

Top Gordon took the Bravos over to tenderly load the bodies onto the back of their truck.

The sergeant sighed. "Well, hell! There ain't much

reason to hang around here. Let's get on to Dak Bla."

"Yeah," Archie said. "There's more war waiting."

CHAPTER 7

Falconi's detachment had one more truck trip to endure after their arrival in Dak Bla. But this particular jaunt was a short one of only twenty minutes up to the nearest point on the Song Cai River.

There was a small military base situated there that was far enough forward to be fortified, while its garrison was kept on a permanent alert status with numerous guard posts. But it was located at a safe distance from unsecured territory, therefore it was never bothered by the raiding done by the Communist river boats.

The three sailors—Chris Hawkins, Chief Brewster, and Blue Richards—leapt down from the back of the truck with wide grins. They could see the three LCPL MK II boats tied up at the dock.

"Damn!" the chief exclaimed. "This here's a happy moment for an old salt. It's like pulling into a home port after years of sea duty."

"Hot damn!" Blue Richards exclaimed to express his joy.

Chris Hawkins, though just as excited, kept his emotions under tight New England control. "It'll be good to have the feel of a deck under my feet again."

A small, thin South Vietnamese Army major, accompanied by a senior non-com, approached them. He displayed a wide grin. "Are you here, Colonel Falconi?" he asked in English.

Falconi stepped forward. *"Toy Trung-Ta* Falconi," he said as a courtesy in Vietnamese.

The major saluted. "I am most pleased to make your acquaintance, sir," He turned and pointed to the boats. "Your ships are arrived and float under the guard of my men at the dock there."

Falconi suppressed a grin at the formal, incorrect English. "What about the American personnel who brought them?"

"Alas!" the major lamented as if a great tragedy had occurred. "They could not stay to attend upon you. They returned forthwith to their base."

"Right. They were a Navy SEAL outfit," Falconi said. "No doubt they've got a busy schedule as it is without delivering boats." The colonel motioned to Chris. "Check 'em out, sailor. If they're—pardon the expression—shipshape, we'll get this show of ours on the road."

"Aye, aye, sir," Chris replied. "C'mon, swabs!" He led the chief and Blue at a trot down to the dock. The trio clambered aboard and began a professional inspection of the craft.

Falconi, followed by the others, sauntered down at a more leisurely pace. The Army men, and most certainly Paulo Garcia, had done their own stint of SCUBA and other amphibious training. But the love of ships, boats and the water just wasn't in their blood like in the Navy's contribution to the Black Eagles. Where most of the detachment saw only three modes of transportation to get them up and down the

77

river, the sailors perceived the craft as entities with souls and hearts; objects which deserved their complete love and affection.

By the time the others reached the dock, the initial inspection was over. "They're not fancy," Chris Hawkins reported. "But they're in fine condition. I can't say much for the engines until a trial run."

"Trial, hell!" Falconi said leaping aboard the lead boat. "We've got orders to take these babies to war—" He winked at the Navy men. "—or as you three would say, 'into harms' way.'"

"Harm's way it is, sir," the chief said. "There is one slight problem that's got us stymied."

"What's that?" Falconi asked concerned.

Chris Hawkins looked over at Hank Valverde. "Weren't these babies supposed to be armed?"

"Right," Hank said. "Quad-fifties to be exact." He glanced over at the boats. "Are they lying on the deck waiting to be mounted?"

"There are none," Chris said. "These craft are unarmed."

"Another fuckup for the Black Eagles," Archie said. "We've had more broken promises than a ugly ol' maid."

Falconi felt a flash of anger. "Well, goddamnit, we can't hold up the mission for that. I'll get on the horn and try to straighten it up. In the meantime, we'll use our own weapons." He motioned to Chief Brewster. "Fire up the engine. Let's test that segment out at least."

The chief stepped up to the control console and punched the engine into life. He pushed forward on the throttle without engaging the clutch. "Tuned tighter'n a mermaid's pussy!" he exclaimed.

Blue Richards leaped over the cockpit to the foredeck and ran to the line holding the boat to the dock. He cast it off.

"What're you waiting for?" Chris called. "Hard to starboard and damn the torpedos!"

"Aye, aye, sir!" the chief shouted back. He spun the wheel to the right and engaged the clutch. The boat leapt to life, turning out into the river, leaving a white wake in the dirty brown water. The bow bit deep as the throttle was pushed forward, and the old sailor came about with such skill that the craft hardly skidded despite the reckless turn.

He brought the boat back to cheers and applause. Falconi got down to business. "Three drivers—"

"Excuse me, sir," Hawkins said. "These are men o' war even if they're small and stuck on an inland river. Let's call the 'drivers' helmsmen."

"Helmsmen it is then," Falconi said agreeably. "We'll have the chief, Blue, and—" He looked around, but there was only one other logical choice. "Paulo."

The Portuguese-American ex-fisherman wasted no time in bounding across the dock and leaping aboard the nearest craft. Blue went to the third. Within a couple of minutes, the three small boats were going through their serious "sea-trials." In only fifteen minutes, all had passed with flying colors.

The only man to keep his cool was the ever logical Hank Valverde. "Any time you jokers want to knock off the fun and games, you can give me a hand loading the extra fuel, chow and ammo. You seemed to have forgotten this ain't a fishing trip we're going on."

"Okay," Falconi said. "One guy from each fire team."

"Calvin," Sergeant Major Gordon called out.

79

"Jesus!" Calvin complained. "Lift and tote! Lift and tote! This place is worse than my old man's sharecropper farm."

"Swift Elk," Chris Hawkins ordered.

"Sure," Swift Elk said. "I'll help out ol' Buffalo Soljer and Hank."

"I'll help too," Malpractice volunteered. "I want to check out the medical goodies anyhow."

While the supply detail loaded the boats, the helmsmen went through the thorough check of their craft under Chris Hawkins's direction. By the time they had finished, the supplies were evenly distributed.

"Let's go," Falconi said. "Alphas get Boat One. The command element will board Boat Two, and the Bravos will be in the rear." He walked over to the second craft where the AN/PRC-41 radio had been set up. "Let's get to the middle of the river. I want to make a commo check."

The chief played easy with the throttle, making a slow run from the dock with both Falconi and Archie Dobbs aboard. The lieutenant colonel took the microphone. "Abner, Abner. This is Falcon. Over." He repeated the call twice more before the answer came back loud and clear.

"Falcon. This is Abner. Message coming. Over."

The chief nudged Archie. "It'll be in code. Get the pad and pencil outta my pack."

Archie quickly complied and barely had time to lay the writing materials on the control console before Station Abner spoke again.

"Message follows. Over."

"This is Falcon. Go ahead. Over," Falconi said.

The speaker began to slowly and distinctly pronounce a series of numbers. Archie copied them down in groups of five as the transmission continued for three full minutes.

Station Abner spoke again. "End of message. Over."

"Roger. Out," Falconi said. He took over the wheel from the chief as the Navy man took the pad from Archie. Then he began deciphering the numbers with the help of his code book. When he finished, he slipped it over to Falconi and happily became a helmsman again.

"Jesus," Falconi said.

"What's up, sir?" Archie asked.

"Evidently we have an asset."

"Good deal," Archie said. "We can sure use some sneaky individual to help us out. Who is it?"

"It's only a code name," Falconi said. "Get over to Boat One, Chief. It looks like we're going to send Swift Elk out into the cold."

Archie winced. "Damn! That sneaky intelligence stuff gives me the willies!" He shrugged. "Oh, well. Want me to go along with him, Skipper?"

Falconi shook his head. "Swift Elk will be doing this work in indigenous civvies complete with a native guide."

"If the VC police him up, they'll shoot him as a spy," the chief said.

Falconi only nodded. "He knew there'd be days like this when he went into S-2 work," he said as the chief brought their boat in close to the Alpha's craft.

SOG Headquarters, located at Peterson Field in Saigon, was where CIA field officer Chuck Fagin spent most of his waking hours—and a hell of a lot of sleeping ones during times he sweated out Black

81

Eagle missions.

He'd looked forward to a few easy days after the hectic activities in preparing for Operation Song Cai Duel. The only thing on his desk had been a bit of paperwork that had piled up. Most of this required signatures and filing—with a couple of bullshit replies to keep the higher echelon boys off his back—then he could prop his feet up and slowly sip scotch-and-sodas until the first reports would begin filtering in from Lieutenant Colonel Falconi.

But those precious few tranquil hours were not to be.

When he checked in at the MP desk in the main reception area, there was a message for him to report to G2 for a special briefing. Usually this was a prelude to being issued an operations plan that would involve the Black Eagles. But since the detachment was already committed, he felt a spasm of dread.

This could mean bad news.

Fagin hurried up to the third floor and went through a series of security checks before he was finally admitted into the hallowed sanctum of SOG G2—Intelligence Branch. He wasted no time with the sergeant in the anteroom. "I'm Fagin. Douglas wants to see me."

"Right," the sergeant said. He buzzed the intercom in a series of prearranged signals. "Go on in."

Fagin walked around the desk and entered a door that led to a short hallway. There was another portal at the end. He went through it without ceremony. "What the hell's going on, Douglas?"

A stocky, bald colonel glanced up from a report he was reading. "Hi, Chuck. Sit down. I got some news that might be a boon to your boy Falconi."

Fagin settled into the chair offered him. "Boon or

boom?"

Colonel Douglas chuckled. "Damn, you're funny." He searched through the manila folders spread around him until he located one. "Here we go." He opened it. "Seems an asset has surfaced in the Song Cai area that will provide valuable information to the Black Eagles."

"What sort of information?"

"Enemy locations, activities, numbers—the whole nine yards," Douglas said. "A gift from heaven, huh?"

"Should I notify Falconi about this immediately, or is the situation still to be developed?" Fagin asked.

"It's already full blown," Douglas said. "And Falconi is in on the know. I personally had a coded message sent to him."

"Goddamnit!" Fagin complained. "I'm supposed to be fully briefed on this stuff from the beginning. Why didn't you call me?"

"Didn't see the point," Douglas said. His eyes narrowed. "Anyhow, I don't report to you." The meaning of the words was loud and clear despite the understatement.

Fagin, irritated, stood up and put his hands on his hips. He leaned forward slightly. "I don't give a damn about who reports to whom. We have a system and an organization set up that is supposed to keep the wheels rolling on these projects. There's so damned many people involved that things get fucked up under the best of circumstances. Look what happened on the last operation."

Douglas, not a bit intimidated, casually tilted back in his swivel chair. "It's the nature of war."

"Nature of war!" Fagin yelled. "Are you forgetting that Falconi and his guys were literally pinned to the

83

side of a jungle cliff? They were out of ammo and ready to make a final bayonet charge, for Chrissake! If it hadn't been for their scout who organized an unauthorized helicopter complete with pilot, there wouldn't be a goddamned Black Eagle detachment right now."

"Yeah. Well, things either work out or they don't."

Fagin's voice quivered with anger. "Listen hard to me, Douglas. I'm getting goddamned sick and tired of the cavalier way you bastards send Falconi and his guys out on limbs while you sit back and sort of hope for the best!"

"*You* listen, Fagin! When—"

"Your half-assed, fucked up planning has cost a detachment which has a TO of eleven men, exactly thirty-three KIA. That's three times their number, you sonofabitch!"

"Shut up, Fagin!" Douglas roared. "Like I said—I don't report to you! And that also means I don't take any shit out of you either."

Fagin knew his rage was useless. He tried to calm down. "That's right, Douglas. You don't take any shit. *I* take the shit. Every time something does wrong and a couple of Black Eagles die, I'm the guy who has to face them. Sometimes it's easy when they're outright nasty about it. But it's tougher when they just look at me with those silent, accusing stares."

"It's your job," Douglas said.

Fagin was silent for several moments. "This is no use." He sighed. "Okay. Okay. They've got an asset. Reliable?"

"We don't know how to rate the snitch," Douglas said. "But I've already ordered contact be made."

Fagin's jaw tightened visibly. "Right. How'd it look?"

"Not bad," Douglas said. "Our agent will take the intelligence sergeant in for an initial interrogation."

"Okay. Who's the asset?"

Douglas grinned. "You'll like this one. She's a whorehouse madame." He checked the folder again. "Name of—Fleurette Hue."

CHAPTER 8

Ray Swift Elk hunched over in the small boat. He was dressed as a native, complete with black pajama-type suit and a *moi cai non*—the conical hat woven of rice—that was so common in the area. Despite the growing darkness of a fast descending dusk, the intelligence sergeant was worried about being spotted as a foreigner. This is why he slumped in order to appear smaller. The copper coloring of his skin helped some, but that aquiline nose that was so prevalent among plains Indians would be a dead giveaway—literally—if some VC happened to be on the river bank and took a close look at him.

The boat Swift Elk rode in was being poled up the river by a South Vietnamese agent named Choy. A native born citizen of Chinese ancestry, Choy, as a young boy, had also served the French in the capacity of spy, courier, informant and general handyman when there were little jobs to be done behind enemy lines or in dangerous areas. It was Choy who had arranged the contact between the Black Eagles and the whore madame Fleurette Hue.

The Chinese-Vietnamese leaned heavily on the pole. "No too far now, G.I.," he said.

Swift Elk nodded. The only weaponry he had on him was a .45 auto in a tanker's shoulder holster under the black shirt he wore. But if this turned out to be a double-cross, it would be enough to blow Choy into the land of his ancestors and take out a couple of other potential baddies who might be around. Any further action after that—such as a successful escape—would have to be played by ear.

Choy gave the boat a slight turn and brought it in to bump gently against the muddy river bank. He motioned Swift Elk to jump ashore, then he followed. After tying up to a tree that leaned out over the water, Choy again signaled to the Sioux Indian. "Come! Come!"

Swift Elk instinctively reached inside the shirt to loosen the pistol in his holster as he followed Choy through the jungle. They only traveled twenty meters before they stopped.

"Wait here," Choy said. "I bring asset to you." He grinned. "Pretty woman. Got whores. Maybe she got more than information for Black Eagle."

Swift Elk only nodded. On intelligence missions, he didn't give a damn if the women he ran into were the legendary spirit maidens of his tribe—this was one warrior who was all business.

Choy winked, then disappeared into the brush. Swift Elk unholstered the .45 and pulled the slide back, letting it ease forward into battery. He was going to be ready in case of any trouble. Then he left the clearing and found a spot that offered good cover in the bushes. There was also an open path back to the boat and the river in case of trouble.

Then he settled down to wait.

Night had come in quietly and darkly onto the village of Tam Nuroc.

Lieutenant Colonel Falconi had set up a perimeter of defense in handy places. Although it was an inconvenience to the villagers, they appreciated his efforts. After the massacre on market day, they were glad to have some heavily armed Americans around. Even if there were only a dozen or so of them.

Alpha Fire Team took the waterfront. With Ray Swift Elk out on an intelligence mission, Archie Dobbs had joined them to fill in the gap. Their M16s, with Paulo Garcia's grenade launcher in a strategic position, covered the small dock where their three LCPL MK II boats were moored.

Sergeant Major Gordon's Bravo Fire Team were on the opposite side of the small hamlet. They'd positioned themselves inside the jungle line, setting up field of fire that could sweep across any avenues of entrance to the village.

Falconi and Chief Brewster ran several commo checks with Abner—SOG's advance operational base—and were satisfied that any signals could be picked up anywhere in the mission area. The next checkout was their private air force.

"Norski. Norski," Falconi said into the microphone. "This is Falcon. Over."

There were only couple of beats of dead air before Warrant Officer Stensland's voice came back. "Falcon. This is Norski. Got a mission? Over."

"Negative," Falconi replied. "Commo check only. How do you read me? Over."

"Five by five," Stensland replied. "Gunnar the Gunner is all primed and so is the Naughty Norski.

You know what we're here for. Over."

Falconi grinned. "Roger that, Norski. Stand by. It'll be a long night for us. But you take a break and get some sleep. Also stay sober. Over."

"War is hell, Falcon. Out."

Chief Brewster was enthusiastic. "Jesus, Skipper. The commo is fantastic around here. That's one thing we won't have to worry about this time."

Falconi nodded. "Yeah." The last mission had been just the opposite. The detachment had been completely cut off almost from the very beginning. From the point of Archie Dobbs's medical evacuation up to the time his voice suddenly boomed at them from Stensland's helicopter, the Black Eagles were operating with absolutely no contact from friendly sources. All this while they were embattled with a bunch of fanatic Algerian camel jockeys.

"It sets your mind easy, don't it, sir?" the chief remarked.

"Yeah," Falconi agreed. "Except right now I'm more than a little concerned about Swift Elk."

A rustling of vegetation alerted the Black Eagles' intelligence sergeant. With an instinct bred into him by countless generations of warriorhood, the Sioux Indian moved silently forward to observe the clearing in front of him.

The moon was brilliant by then, lighting up that particular area like daylight although the jungle around was dark as ever. Choy stepped into view. He whispered the pre-arranged code word aloud. "Tiger. Tiger. Tiger."

Swift Elk gritted his teeth. This was the hairiest part of intelligence work. It was a situation where he couldn't hang back. He had to put his life on the line.

The Black Eagle stepped out into the clearing.

Choy hurried forward and a slight figure scurried behind him. They stopped and the agent made a quick introduction. "Here is asset. Name of Fleurette." He pointed to the sergeant. "Here is G.I. Name of Injun." He used Swift Elk's working code name.

Swift Elk nodded and took a close look at the woman. She was, indeed, beautiful. Although obviously a mature woman, Fleurette Hue still had the delicate loveliness so unique to Asian females. "You have information for us?"

Fleurette nodded. "I have pleasure house. North Vietnam boat soldier come there."

Swift Elk noted the Freudian slip, but displayed no amusement. "Do they talk much about what they do?" His extensive training had taught him to speak in the simplest terms when dealing with foreign assets and other personnel. This avoided misunderstandings on both sides.

"Yes. I know one boat go to Tam Nuroc tomorrow. They want to look at the village. They want to know if soldiers there."

Swift Elk knew she meant a reconnaissance mission. "Why do you tell me this?"

"I want you to win the war," Fleurette said.

Swift Elk pressed on. "Why?"

"I lose pleasure house in Saigon," Fleurette explained. "Whore boss there no let me have business. But long time ago I have one in Hanoi for French. That my city. Not Saigon. You win war, I go back there to my city."

Swift Elk's quick mind analyzed this particular asset. No patriotic or ideological motives. That was good. Sometimes such persons are fanatics and end up causing more grief than good work on a mission.

Also, most double-agents will play up to both sides' political aims in an instinctive gesture of ingratiation. But someone who unabashedly said they were performing services for monetary gains, could be trusted up to a point.

"Will you give us all information you hear?" Swift Elk asked.

"Yes," Fleurette replied.

"*All* of it?"

"Yes."

"What about the girls in your house? Will they help us too?"

Fleurette shook her head. "Not good girls. Cheap girls. Dumb girls. So work in country."

"Can you write numbers and letters in English?"

"No. In French," Fleurette said.

"That's all right," Swift Elk said. He knew that Lt. Chris Hawkins had studied French at Annapolis. On the other hand, Falconi himself was fluent in Vietnamese. "If you have something very complicated to say, write in your own language." He preferred everything in French if only for the slight chance of casual observers who might find a message being unable to read it.

"I will remember to do that," Fleurette said.

"Okay," Swift Elk said. "We cannot visit your pleasure house because it is too far into enemy territory. But we can sneak into here." He pointed toward the river. "There is a big tree there that leans way out over the water. It is easy to see. When you want to tell us something, write it down and put it under the roots at the base of that tree."

"Yes. I can do that."

"Do you take many walks around here?"

"Yes," Fleurette replied. "Many times I walk to here and back to my house."

91

"Good," Swift Elk said. At least she wouldn't attract any undue attention if she wanted to come down and leave them some information. "We will leave you money there too."

"I don't need money," Fleurette said. "I want to go to Hanoi."

"Okay. When we win the war, you can go to Hanoi. I promise," Swift Elk said although he knew he couldn't guarantee what he said in the slightest. Another part of intelligence work was to be a lying sonofabitch. "Thank you for telling us about the boat. Don't forget that tree. Goodby."

"Goodby," Fleurette said. She bowed slightly, then turned and hurried away down the dark path.

Swift Elk grabbed Choy's shoulder. "Let's get back to Tam Nuroc."

"Okay, G.I.! North Vietnamese not know you there. Big surprise for that boat." He hurried back toward the river.

"I hope it doesn't turn out to be a big surprise for us," Swift Elk said following him.

Although the village militia of Tam Nuroc were at their regular sentry posts, Falconi had also set up a guard detail of Black Eagles. No one, individually or collectively, could be trusted on this particular mission.

Archie Dobbs, farther forward than the rest of the Alpha Team guard detail, heard the gentle disturbance in the usual noise patterns of the slowly flowing river. He brought his M16 up and sighted toward the dark shape approaching him. Alerted for Swift Elk's return, he allowed the stranger to come up within whispering distance.

"I love you," he challenged.

92

"Forever," came back Swift Elk's voice with the password.

Archie made kissing sounds with his lips.

"Asshole!" Swift Elk said as the boat glided past the sentry post and on toward the dock. Choy brought them in between two of the Black Eagles' war launches. Swift Elk leaped onto the wooden platform, then hurried to the newly established headquarters in the middle of the village. Choy scrambled after him, having trouble keeping up with his long strides.

Falconi didn't hide his relief at seeing him. "I've been sweating this out."

Swift Elk grinned. "Me too, Skipper. But we might really be onto something here."

"Good source," Choy added.

"The only problem is distance and location," Swift Elk said. "But I've arranged a deadletter drop at a certain tree on the river bank. It leans way over the water, so it's easy to spot. We can send Choy there, or have one of us make a sneak-and-peek run up that way to check for information."

"I'm going to have to arrange for funds," Falconi said. "What does this asset want in the way of repayment?"

"Nothing," Swift Elk replied. "She wants a promise that when we win the war she can set up a whorehouse in Hanoi."

"Mmm," Falconi mused. "No monetary or political motivations here? What's your assessment?"

"Go easy," Swift Elk advised. "We've got the makings of a real double-agent here. She could be playing both sides for all she can get."

Chief Brewster winked at him. "Did you give her gals a trial run, Ray?"

Swift Elk grinned. "Hell, no. She said they weren't

worth much."

"Yeah," the chief said. "Prob'ly real dawgs. That's why they're working way out here in the boonies."

"We'll be able to test our her information real soon," Swift Elk said. "She says there's an NVA recon boat coming down here tomorrow afternoon."

"Good," Falconi said. "We might as well let the bastards know we're here. The sooner the fighting starts, the sooner the mission ends." He turned to Choy. "I want you to avoid Tam Nuroc for a while except at night."

Choy nodded in understanding. "Right. I go back up river for a few days anyhow. See what I can learn."

"Good man," Falconi said. "We appreciate your help."

"Hey," Choy said grinning. "You buy me a good time in that Hanoi whorehouse after war won, eh?" He walked to the door. "See you later, G.I."

Falconi watched him leave, then turned to the chief. "Fetch Chris and Top for me, will you, Chief? We've got an ambush to plan."

CHAPTER 9

Blue Richards and Calvin Culpepper, both stripped buck-assed naked, dove off the boat into the muddy waters of the Song Cai. The other Black Eagles standing at the gunwale and on the foredeck grinned at the ludicrous sight.

Spitting and hacking, the swimmers' heads broke the surface as they came up for air. The silty water was thick in their hair and dripped down their faces leaving brown streaks.

"This is some cruddy river," Calvin complained as they swam back to the hull of the craft.

"Yeah," Blue agreed, "but if this here Song Cai was back home, it'd be chock full of some big ol' channel catfish."

Top Gordon was bit impatient. "You guys knock off the chatter and get to work," he said.

"Hup, Sarge!" Calvin said as he and Blue put their hands on the boat and began pushing against it while paddling like hell with their feet.

While the rest of the Black Eagles on board gave quiet encouragement, the LCPL MK II moved slowly and reluctantly in toward the bank, slipping beneath the overhanging vegetation that hung down to the water's surface from jungle trees. As soon as the boat was behind cover, Top Gordon leaned over the gunwale and grasped Blue in his brawny grip.

"Alley oop!" he grunted as he pulled him up. He repeated the chore for Calvin, dragging him dripping onto the deck.

The two took a couple of towels and wiped themselves as dry as possible. The effort left the large G.I. terrycloths dirty and blotchy. Blue looked at his when he'd finished. "This thing is flat ruined."

"Might as well throw 'em away," Calvin agreed. "Unless we can find some fast-running fresh water to soak 'em in for a couple of days."

"Snap it up," Top said.

They quickly dressed while Malpractice McCorckel and Archie Dobbs spread freshly-hacked foliage across the foredeck and the port side of the small vessel.

When they'd finished, Lieutenant Colonel Falconi was pleased with the effect. "Anybody would have to know exactly where we are if they were to spot us," he said.

"Yes, sir," Top agreed. "I just hope that asset that Swift Elk got his intelligence from is reliable."

"Good point," Archie Dobbs said. "If the bitch was setting us up, there'll be a gunboat showing up instead of a recon craft."

The thought of being blown out of the water through treachery and deceit had already occurred to Falconi. That was the main reason he had decided to use only one of their own boats. He'd chosen Top Gordon's Fire Team Bravo—reinforced by himself and Archie Dobbs—to test Fleurette Hue's reliability.

Calvin Culpepper wiped at his wet face. He'd begun sweating, making salty streaks down his muddy features. "Shit! We'll never dry off in this humidity."

"Maybe we shoulda brung some more towels, huh?" Blue Richards mused.

Top shook his head. "Wouldn't have done you any good. And they'd just have gotten muddy like the others anyhow."

"And I thought we had some silty water in Alabama," Blue said in disgust.

"They tell me the Mississippi in Louisiana is pretty dirty," Calvin remarked.

Although they were speaking in soft whispers, Falconi didn't like the unnecessary chatter. "Knock it off, guys," he cautioned them. "We don't want some VC foot patrol hearing us. It's time to squat and listen for our expected visitor."

With rifles already locked-and-loaded, the group settled down for what many combat veterans consider the worst part of an ambush—anticipatory waiting.

Archie, stretched out across the foredeck, barely breathed as he strained his ears for the sound of the approaching enemy launch.

It wasn't long before the local insect population discovered the waiting men. The first bouts of irritating buzzing finally grew to a barely discernible but steady hum of flapping bug wings as the pests darted around then landed on bare flesh to feed on warm blood.

The Black Eagles didn't dare slap the insects. The sound of a loud whack would travel hundreds of meters both up and down the river. They killed the irritating little bastards as best they could by squashing them.

"Hssst!" Archie hissed through his teeth.

They forgot about the bites and stings as all ears strained for whatever it was that had alerted Archie.

Within moments the distant sound of a marine engine could be heard. The noise grew slowly louder, and Blue Richards made a sailor's observation. "She's goin' 'bout quarter-speed, I reckon. I'd say the skipper o' that craft ain't in much of a hurry."

"That should extend his life span by a few minutes," Falconi remarked coldly.

Calvin Culpepper, the grenadier, assumed a squatting position by the gunwale. The M203 was cocked and ready to launch an M397 airburst round. Falconi had figured the enemy crew would be knocked out of action quicker that way.

Suddenly Archie looked back at them. "Here she comes, boys!"

There was no need for noise discipline now. The sound of the motor would drown out any bit of racket they made.

Archie got the first good view. "There's seven bad guys on board," he announced. "Get ready, Calvin!"

Calvin Culpepper waited for the exact moment, then he pulled the trigger. But a slight swell in the water caused the Red boat to roll slightly, so that when the 40-millimeter round hit, it glanced off into the jungle before exploding.

"Shit!" Calvin swore. He quickly reloaded.

"There they go!" Blue yelled. He rushed to the control console and fired up the engine as the North Vietnamese helmsman made a frantic port-about maneuver.

Archie almost slid off the foredeck as the Bravo Boat whipped out of its cover and headed upriver after the escaping Red.

Calvin kicked off another round, but the Communist helmsman was no amateur. He was already weaving violently across the water. The small missile whipped past the enemy on the starboard side, smacked the water, then tumbled across the river's surface before exploding harmlessly fifty meters ahead of the target.

Archie fired several full-automatic bursts. Then the foredeck exploded into splinters of laminated fiberglass around him.

"Jesus!" Archie yelled. "The sonofabitch has a heavy machine gun pointing backwards!"

"That's astern," Blue Richards said, calmly correcting his friend's terminology.

Archie was not amused. He scrambled back toward the cockpit. "Excuse me all to hell, Blue!" he sneered as automatic fire beat the air around his ears. "I ain't up to all that swabby talk." He dove across the console and crashed to the deck.

In the meantime, Falconi, Top and Malpractice were sweeping the area to the front with overlapping sprays of M16 fire. But the incoming enemy rounds finally forced Blue to do his own bit of evasive piloting.

Without a steady platform to work from, the Black Eagles' accuracy went from bad to shitty as they swung back and forth under Blue's helmsmanship.

"Goddamnit!" Falconi swore furiously. "I wish we had gotten those quad-fifties like we were promised."

Calvin Culpepper, never one to give up, valiantly exposed himself to the NVA machine gun with each effort to deliver an effective grenade.

Blue fought the wheel. "I don't wanna upset none o' y'all, but if we git many more hits on the hull we're gonna sink."

"No sweat," Archie said. "Ever'body knows how to swim."

"You crazy-assed Yankee!" Blue exclaimed. "You think that sumbitch is just gonna watch us paddle over to the bank? He'll whup that craft o' his around and come back gunning hard and heavy."

The Bravo Boat shook under another pounding of automatic fire.

"Oh, man, shit!" Blue cursed as he fought to control the careening vessel.

The Black Eagles continued shooting at what had become an impossible target. The only advantage to that was the fact it was just as hard for the NVA gunner up ahead to hit them too. His rounds—big 12.7 millimeter slugs from a Russian DShK heavy machine gun—whipped heavily through the air around them.

But Calvin Culpepper stood in the middle of the boat and rocked in time with its movements. Finally he felt the time was right and he squeezed off another airburst grenade that went so close to Blue's head that he ducked.

"Watch it!" Blue complained. But he shut up quickly when the small missile hit the stern of the Red boat. It went five feet straight up into the air, then exploded.

The NVA gunner and two more of his friends were slammed down in the hail of steel. The big machine gun spun wildly in its mounted stand, its belt wrapping around the careening weapon.

The force of the blast almost broached the boat, and the helmsman fought hard to turn it back into its original direction of travel.

But it cost him time.

Blue, seizing the opportunity, pushed forward on the throttle. The Bravo Team's craft leaped forward and quickly closed the gap between the two launches. The Black Eagles' rifle fire knocked down two more NVAs. One somersaulted over the gunwale and hit the river, making a muddy splash.

Calvin fired again. This time he'd gone for a dual

purpose round that was armor piercing. The projectile slammed through the transom and exploded. The Red craft went dead in the water.

But not its crew. Surprisingly, neither seemed injured.

The helmsman knew his craft was sinking, but he was a fighter. He rushed back to the heavy machine gun and swung the muzzle around. Already cocked, all he had to do was work the trigger to send a stream of heavy bullets streaking toward the Bravo Boat. His buddy's AK47 added to the flying slugs. Blue had gotten the Black Eagle launch in too close for any evasive maneuvering or retreating.

All he could do was charge ahead.

The Bravo Boat closed in, its port side deck raked by bullets. Then the Black Eagles streaked past the enemy craft, and Blue spun the wheel to starboard. He let out a wild, Rebel yell.

His comrades-in-arms took the hint. Calvin Culpepper forgot the M203 and reverted to rifleman. Falconi and Malpractice stayed on full auto while the other three rifles pumped away with individual shots.

"They're abandonin' ship!" Blue called. He disengaged the clutch and pulled back on the throttle. The Bravo Boat slid past the Red craft, putting it between them and the two NVAs who had left their sinking vessel to swim for shore.

"Let's get a couple of prisoners," Falconi ordered.

"Aye, aye, sir," Blue said. He eased the boat forward fast enough to catch up to the desperately swimming men.

The two NVAs instinctively hunched their shoulders as they expected to be blasted in the back.

"Dung so!" Falconi yelled out assuring them they wouldn't be slaughtered. *"Hang di!"*

The two, almost relieved, did as they had just been

101

ordered.

They surrendered.

The moon was bright over the village of Tam
Nuroc. Although a lantern wasn't necessary, one
hissed in the hut where the NVA prisoner squatted on
the floor.

Lt. Col. Robert Falconi, playing an interrogator's
role, sat on a chair looking down at the man. This
wasn't from discourtesy. It put the prisoner at a
psychological disadvantage. He was forced into a
submissive position whether he liked it or not. He
had to look up into Falconi's face to communicate
with him.

The American had already complimented the POW
on his job as helmsman that afternoon. Speaking
fluent Vietnamese, he laughed. "You almost got away
from us, soldier."

The prisoner said nothing.

"Where did you learn your skill with a boat?"
Falconi said pleasantly. "We were certainly im-
pressed!"

Silence.

"Are you from a town or village near a river? Or
perhaps even the sea?" Falconi said. He pulled a
cigarette from him pocket. *Moi ong hut thuoc?*

The enemy soldier licked his lips, then slowly
reached out and took the smoke. He inhaled hungrily
after Falconi had lit it for him. Then he went back to
his brooding stare.

"Listen, please," Falconi said. "I really don't wish
to be a bother, but I would like to ask you some
questions." He followed this with a few general
inquiries into the man's rank, unit, and other minor
matters. But the prisoner wouldn't answer. *"Xin loi*

ong," Falconi said apologetically. "But you really must tell me what you know. My partner is a very unpleasant man. If I do not get information from you, he will scold me and take over the questioning himself."

The POW sullenly exhaled the smoke and said nothing. But he looked up at the entrance of a newcomer. His eyes widened slightly at the sight of Ray Swift Elk.

The Sioux looked menacing in the lantern light. His expression scowled at the prisoner. Then he and Falconi exchanged angry words in English, and the lieutenant colonel left the hut.

Swift Elk's questioning was very different from Falconi's. He yelled and threatened, working himself into a fit that made the prisoner break out into a cold sweat. After a half hour of this, Falconi returned.

Again there was an angry exchange. Swift Elk glared at the prisoner, then stalked angrily out of the hut.

Falconi gave the man another cigarette. "You really must talk. He is only giving me one more chance with you."

The man was clearly nervous, but he only gritted his teeth. After a quarter of an hour, Falconi called for a guard. Archie appeared and took the prisoner away. A couple of minutes later, the second NVA appeared under Calvin Culpepper's custody.

Falconi hollered and cursed at the man trying to get him to talk until Chris Hawkins came in. The same game was played again, this time with Falconi leaving. Chris became the nice guy, offering some hot tea from his canteen as he begged the man to talk before the unpleasant colonel returned.

This "Mutt-and-Jeff" technique took several hours before there were any results. It was dawn by the time

103

Swift Elk was able to make an accurate intelligence summary of the two POWs.

"They're a couple of meatheads, sir," he reported to the colonel. "Neither one of 'em knows the area or much about their unit. I'd say they wasn't lying when they said they'd only been assigned for a couple of weeks."

"Do you think they were sacrifices?" Falconi asked his intelligence expert.

"It's possible," Swift Elk allowed. "If that whore lady is a double agent, then she could have set this up with the Red commander to put our minds at ease where she's concerned."

Falconi was thoughtful for several moments before he spoke. "This is the kind of war I hate the worst," he said angrily.

"Yeah," Swift Elk agreed. "This here's the classic situation to get shot in the back."

CHAPTER 10

The headquarters of the North Vietnamese Army's 4th Boat Rifle Battalion was located in a snug little area on the Song Cai about twenty kilometers north of Tam Nuroc.

The site had been picked strictly for security, but it was a pleasant place to be, too. There was a wide bend in the river which made an excellent observation post. Great distances of the waterway, both north and south, could be kept under constant, easy surveillance. It would be impossible for anyone to pull a sneak attack on the post.

The recently constructed huts that served as headquarters and living accommodations for the battalion were spread throughout the palm trees in the vicinity. All excess brush had been cut away — and kept that way — while a daily work crew swept and wet the ground until it was hardpacked and smooth as a wood floor.

The jungle around it also offered security. Dense and tangled, the natural barricade was further strengthened by the presence of several very active Viet Cong units that prowled the operational area.

Therefore, the unit commander, Captain Ngy, felt reasonably sure that no force short of a full-fledged regiment with supporting artillery would be able to penetrate his mission territory. And even if it did, he could still get away since it would be impossible to surprise him in his lair.

It was a bit past mid-morning when Ngy stood at the river bank. Here the water was deep enough to offer a natural anchorage for his unit's boats. A crudely constructed floating dock jutted out for them to moor on. The captain watched as one of the craft slowly approached, its commander poised on the bow to leap off at the first opportunity.

When he hit the dock, it sank a bit, then came back to the surface. The young officer hurried across its unstable surface until he reached his commander. He saluted sharply. "I have a report on the missing reconnaissance boat, sir," he announced grimly.

"Please proceed, Comrade Lieutenant."

"It has been destroyed approximately ten kilometers from here," the young lieutenant said. "We found five cadavers floating in the vicinity of the sunken boat. We pulled them from the river and have returned with our dead comrades. But there are two men missing. We could find no trace of them."

"Their bodies undoubtedly floated away," Ngy mused.

"We looked carefully for them, Comrade Captain. But could find nothing. Perhaps they are prisoners."

Ngy nodded. "That is possible. But the cadavers could have floated in close to the bank and become entangled in jungle growth." He walked back toward his headquarters hut with the other officer beside him. "I presume you found no enemy dead."

"Only our own martyred comrades," the lieutenant said. "Any corpses of capitalist running dogs were

106

undoubtedly taken away by the surviving gangsters."

"Of course," Ngy agreed. "Could you tell what caused our craft to sink?"

"An explosion, Comrade Captain," the lieutenant said. "We recovered numerous pieces of the boat that had shrapnel damage, and there were several large areas burned by flashes."

"Yes," Ngy agreed. "That would be ample evidence of a rocket or grenade. Was there other damage?"

"Bullet holes," the lieutenant said.

Ngy, although he had not seen the destroyed boat, could accurately assess what happened. "This was no ambush from the river bank," he said. "Or else our men would have run through it. Another boat had to have engaged them in a fight that consumed much time." He glanced over the shoulder of his companion. "I see your men are bringing the dead comrades ashore."

The lieutenant's jaw tightened with anger. "We never leave our dead, Comrade Captain."

"Correct," Ngy agreed. "And we always avenge them."

The other officer glanced over where the bodies had been respectfully laid out. "They were new men, were they not, Comrade Captain?"

"Yes. I fear they were not experienced enough to defeat the criminals who attacked them," Ngy said.

"I only wish we could have determined who had done this deed!"

"It was undoubtedly a new unit," Ngy said calmly. "The previous South Vietnamese formation showed little desire to come this far north."

"Are you sure?"

Ngy smiled slightly. "Of course, Comrade. There is nothing that happens on the Song Cai that can escape my observation."

107

"*Tot!* When do we avenge our dead comrades?"

"Very soon, Comrade Lieutenant," Ngy said. "Please put the troops on full alert. I want all boats fueled and their armaments fully loaded and inspected. We will go to blast those interlopers off the Song Cai."

The young lieutenant saluted. "I respectfully request that my boat be allowed to lead the assault force."

"Permission granted," Ngy said. "Now to your duties."

The lieutenant, his face locked in a determined, angry expression, turned and rushed away. He shouted orders that brought the troops out of their huts. Ngy knew that within minutes, his small flotilla would be ready to seek out and destroy the newcomers who had snapped at the bait he'd dangled before them.

Chuck Fagin paced in front of the ordnance sergeant's desk, chewing on the stub of stogie that he gripped between his teeth. The sergeant glanced up from his paperwork. "You might as well sit down, Fagin. You know how long them meetings go on."

Fagin took out the stogie and used it to point in the NCO's face. "Damnit, Brannigan! Did you tell Kelsey I wanted to see him ASAP?"

"Sure I did. I told him just like you wanted me to," Sergeant Brannigan said.

"Then why the hell didn't he wait for me?"

"Jesus, Fagin! When a brigadier general calls a meeting, a major's got to go to it, don't he? I mean he can't say, 'Sorry, General, but my ol' pal Fagin wants to see me first'."

"He coulda thought of something," Fagin fumed.

He pointed again with the cigar. "Hell, *you* shoulda thought o' something!"

"Get off my back, Fagin." Brannigan went back to his paperwork.

The two were in the office of SOG's chief ordnance supply officer. This was Major Kelsey, a man who ordinarily could produce any sort of weaponry from exotic heavy stuff right down to small caliber pistols that could be concealed in a man's hatband. But he'd fallen woefully short in his duties where the Black Eagles were concerned. This was Fagin's primary concern, and he'd been waiting more than an hour to see the major.

Brannigan, now really irritated, gave up trying to concentrate on his administrative task. "Gimme a break, Fagin!"

"Go get Kelsey for me then."

"Fuck you! I ain't storming into no officer meeting and dragging a major out to see you—CIA or no CIA!"

Fagin walked over to the desk and leaned on it. He affected a smile. "Then, please, Brannigan, tell me where the meeting is."

Brannigan shook his head. "Not on your life! Major Kelsey said you wasn't to find out in no way where he went." The sergeant grinned. "He knows you're the kinda asshole who'd go over there and make a scene."

"No, I wouldn't."

"Yes, you would. And I ain't telling you nothing. So relax."

Any further comment from Fagin was interrupted when the door opened and Kelsey walked in. The major motioned to the CIA officer. "I figure you'd still be here. C'mon in."

Brannigan assumed an indignant expression. "He

109

tried to get me to tell where you was, sir. But I didn't say nothing."

"Right," Fagin agreed. "He was a perfect asshole. I see why he's your NCO. You two form such a perfect match." He hurried after the officer. "When are you lovers gonna get married?"

Kelsey led the way into his inner office. "Sit down. I know why you're here, and the answer is the same. I can't do a damned thing for you."

"I need heavy weapons, Kelsey. Quad-fifties or at least some individual fifties."

"I have no authorization," Kelsey said.

"I'll sign for 'em myself," Fagin offered.

"Big deal!" Kelsey scoffed. "You don't have the proper funds to transfer over to me. Anyhow, I could never justify working outside of channels."

"The Black Eagles belong to SOG!" Fagin shouted. "You're the SOG ordnance officer. It ain't like they were in the Lower Slobovian army or something."

"Let me try to explain it to you," Kelsey said patiently. "When Falconi and his boys were assigned to Nui Dep, they were put under the administrative umbrella of 5th Special Forces."

"Sure! For billets and chow—"

"—and bullets and guns and rocks or anything else that can be used for weaponry," Kelsey said interrupting the interruption.

"But this mission on the Song Cai wasn't set up that way," Fagin said. "The 5th is already heavily committed to support their own little forays. They don't have anything available to give to Falconi."

"That's something you should have checked as part of your pre-mission activities," Kelsey said.

"Goddamnit all to hell, Kelsey!" Fagin shouted. "It never occurred to me that there'd be a stupid snafu based on supply protocol."

110

Kelsey shrugged. "That's the way the army works."

"Stupid fucking Army!" Fagin growled.

"Listen, Fagin!" Kelsey said menacingly. "I like this 'stupid fucking' Army, and as long as I'm in it, I'll do things its way. And until this red tape is straightened out, I'm not giving a damned thing to Falconi's detachment."

"The mission will be over by the time it would take to wade through that administrative snarl," Fagin protested. "Or the Black Eagles will be floating face down in the Song Cai River."

"Go away, Fagin."

"Those guys are out there on river boats with just their M16s, Kelsey," Fagin said.

"I'm busy."

"The NVAs they're going up against are toting heavy machine guns and rocket launchers," Fagin continued.

"I got work to do," Kelsey said.

"Every time those poor bastards go out on ops, they're sent a day late and a dollar short," Fagin said.

"They're volunteers, Fagin," Kelsey said. "Besides, they blame you for all their troubles, and they don't appreciate the things you get accomplished—which I happen to know are considerable."

"They need someone to hate," Fagin said. "If they knew there were unknown entities—like you—fucking them up, they'd go crazy. As long as they got some dumb bastard like me to point their accusing fingers at, they'll stay on an even keel and do the job we want them to do."

Kelsey gritted his teeth. "I'm sorry."

Fagin relaxed. "Okay. Okay. I know you can't do anything for us. I just thought you might bend a little—hell, I mean a whole lot." He walked to the door, then paused and turned around. "I'm glad

111

you're in the Army now instead of back in 1776, Kelsey. You probably wouldn't have issued blankets to Washington's troops at Valley Forge without the proper paperwork."

"That's right," Kelsey said coldly. "Not even a spool of fucking thread."

"And you'd be an ordnance officer in the frigging colonial army instead of the sovereign United States of America."

"Get outta here, Fagin!" Kelsey yelled.

Fagin left the office.

Ngy had just finished inspecting the three boats he'd chosen for the assault.

His adjutant, an eager young officer who had recently graduated from the NVA's infantry academy, sought him out to personally inform him of an important visitor. This person, known only by the code name "Tho May," was waiting in Ngy's headquarters.

Ngy wasted no time in rushing back to greet the caller. He didn't even bother to take off his pith helmet when he entered his thatched roof office. "*Chao ong*, Comrade," Ngy greeted him.

"*Chao ong*," Tho May replied. "I have hurried here because of the intelligence I bear."

"I appreciate your consideration," Ngy said. "It grieved me much to sacrifice a boat and crew — even if they were newcomers to my unit."

"But it was necessary," Tho May said. "It would whet the Americans' appetites for more action and give them a sense of false security."

"Americans!" Ngy exclaimed. "Is it true we are facing *Nguroi My*? If so, I must quickly inform my men. Such news will assuredly to raise their fighting

112

ardor."

"Indeed," Tho May replied. "We have not yet identified the unit, but we soon shall. At the moment I believe they are a well-trained Army Special Forces or Navy Seal team detachment."

"How long will it take to confirm their identification?" Ngy asked.

"Of course I cannot give you the full information on the spying operation. But the situation is now controlled through a double agent program," Tho May said. "Contact has already been made. When that person is certain who you face, the information will be passed on to me. Naturally, I will waste no time in informing you."

Ngy felt impatient now. "You spoke of special intelligence for me, Comrade."

"*Chac-chan*," Comrade," Tho May said. "The Americans are preparing to move up the river and seek you out."

"Interesting," Ngy said. "How many boats and personnel involved?"

"There are three boats, Comrade, and eleven men."

"We are an entire battalion strung up and down the Song Cai!" Ngy said with a laugh. "What do those idiots hope to do?"

Tho May's face became serious. "The double agent reports they display a great amount of skill and organization, Comrade. There is no doubt they are a special group of soldiers."

"What about their armaments?" Ngy inquired in a concerned voice.

Tho May relaxed his solemn expression and smiled. "They are only armed with M16 rifles and two grenade launchers."

Ngy laughed aloud. "We have heavy machine guns and rockets. They will not stand a chance against us."

113

"Then you plan a sortie against them soon?"

"Since they are coming tomorrow, we will not disappoint them," Ngy said. "I will personally lead three heavily armed boats against them." Then he was thoughtful for a few moments. "On the other hand, since a trap was baited with a launch of riflemen, I should continue the deception with another to draw them into our main force."

"You know best, Comrade." Tho May's grin increased. "Perhaps, then, it is not worth the effort to identify their detachment."

Ngy rubbed his hands together. "You are undoubtedly correct. They will be nothing but rubble and corpses in another twenty-four hours. Who cares about the unit designation of a group of dead men floating in a muddy river?"

CHAPTER 11

Lt. Col. Robert Falconi stood beside Chief Brewster at the control console of the command boat.

The SEAL chief petty officer skillfully guided the craft along against the current of the river in a manner so natural that it was nearly instinctive.

Falconi picked up the mike of the AN/PRC-41 radio. "Naughty Norski. Naughty Norski. This is Falcon. Over."

Chief Warrant Officer Stensland's voice, distorted by his helicopter radio, came on the air. "Falconi. This is Naughty Norski. Over."

"What's your position? Over."

"We're orbiting a few klicks behind you," Stensland replied. "Every time we catch sight of you guys, we draw back. But we're close enough if you need us. Over."

"Roger, Naughty Norski. You're our ace-in-the-hole. So hang in there," Falconi said. "Out." He returned the mike to the radio and gave his full attention to the situation at hand.

Archie Dobbs, his M16 ready for action, crouched at the gunwale, his alert eyes peering into the dark green jungle-entangled banks that they eased past.

"Damn, Skipper," Archie said. "I'd feel better if I was up there on the Alpha boat with Chris and his guys."

Falconi looked over and grinned at his scout. "You've been point man in this outfit so long you feel like a virgin in a whorehouse back here in the middle don't you?"

"It ain't natural for me," Archie acknowledged. He glanced back over the stern and gave a little wave to Blue Richards who was helmsman on the Bravo boat.

"We're a floating command post," Falconi reminded him. The Black Eagle commander now held a Prick-6 radio in one hand and a pair of binoculars in the other. "And since trouble can come at us from any direction, we have to be in position to call the shots from all angles."

"I just hope Paulo Garcia don't get us lost," Archie said in irritation.

Both Falconi and Chief Brewster laughed aloud. The Navy man spoke without taking his eyes from the front. "What the hell do you think Paulo's gonna do? Run up on the river bank and start traveling inland?"

"Okay! Okay!" Archie snapped. "So you can't wander around in circles following a river. I realize that. Still, there's a certain amount of navigating that's gotta be done."

"He has a compass," Falconi assured him. The colonel put the binoculars to his eyes and scanned both sides of the bank.

"Another thing," Archie said continuing to complain. "These here engines make too much noise. How are we supposed to sneak up on anybody?"

"You're in a mechanized, waterborne war, ol' buddy," the chief said.

A rattle of small arms fire broke out ahead before

116

Archie could make a reply.

Immediately, Chris Hawkins' voice came over the Prick-6 radio. "Falcon, this is Alpha. We've made contact."

"What've you got, Alpha?" Falconi asked.

"One boat of riflemen," Chris reported back over the air. "We're moving in now to take 'em. Over."

"Go to it," Falconi urged him. "Out."

The firing built up to a crashing crescendo before the command boat reached the scene. Falconi had ordered Top Gordon to act as rear security during the operation. Blue Richards ran the Bravo boat slowly back and forth across the river while his teammates kept a sharp eye on the bank and to the rear for any interlopers.

The enemy boat was in reverse, but the rate of rifle fire coming from it caused Chris to order Paulo to approach with caution. Ray Swift Elk and Hank Valverde, in the meantime, kept up a steady rate of fire at the NVA craft in hopes of keeping its occupants' heads down and reduce their chances of being able to effectively operate their vessel.

Meanwhile, Chief Brewster brought the command boat to a point off the Alpha's port bow. This gave Falconi and Archie a good opportunity to pour in fire to aid Chris Hawkins and his team in their efforts.

Then the explosion hit the water.

A geyser, thirty feet in height, erupted from the river. The concussion from the blast swept over the Alpha boat, rocking it violently.

"Another enemy boat coming up!" Chris reported over the radio. "Heavily armed!"

Falconi yelled at the chief. "Take us over to the right side of the Alpha's. I want to take a look at what's approaching."

"The starboard side, aye, aye, sir!" the chief said as

117

he spun the wheel and leaned on the throttle.

Two more explosions hit the river. This time the Alpha's craft almost capsized, but managed to right itself. Falconi correctly figured they'd been suckered in by the first enemy vessel. He hollered into the Prick-6. "Alpha! Pull out. Bravo, cover us. We're hauling ass!"

Blue Richards swung his launch to port and headed toward the action. Top Gordon, Malcomb McCorckel and Calvin Culpepper aimed the muzzles of their M16s forward. Calvin's included the M203 grenade launcher. When they closed in, he cut loose with a shot that sent a high explosive grenade lobbing through the air in a lazy trajectory.

It landed dead center in the first NVA boat. The explosion whipped three hundred-plus hunks of shrapnel through the crew. One, the closest to detonation, was blown overboard looking like a spinning hunk of butchered meat. The others went down like scythed wheat without a yell or word of protest.

"Nice shootin', Calvin!" Blue yelled out in admiration.

Never one to rest on his laurels, Calvin pumped off another at the second enemy craft. This one missed, going into the water and exploding about five feet below the surface. All it did was rock the vessel, and the enemy pushed on toward them.

Chief Brewster, on the command boat, finally got a good look at what they were up against. "She's heavily armed, sir," he announced to Falconi. "I see a large caliber machine gun over the windshield, and rocket launchers both port and starboard."

"There's another just like that sonofabitch coming up behind him!" Archie yelled.

"And one more," Falconi said setting his binoculars down. "That's three of the bastards loaded for bear."

"They're set for bear and we're toting stuff to get quail," Archie complained.

Suddenly two more explosions ripped through the air.

"Oh, shit!" Archie yelled at the sight in front of them.

The Alpha boat reared bow-up like a child's toy in a bathtub. But this time it kept going over with its frantic crew reacting to the sudden situation as best they could. Swift Elk and Hank Valverde leaped clear and hit the water. Chris Hawkins and Paulo Garcia, both by the control console, hung on as their launch went completely over until it lay upside down on the water.

"Sonofabitch!" Falconi cursed. He grabbed the radio. "Bravo, cover us! We're going to the Alphas."

"Wilco," came Top's voice as calm as if they were on a Sunday outing at a lake in some park back home.

Archie needed no instructions. He pushed his selector to full auto and started hosing at the enemy while Chief Brewster roared toward the Alpha boat. When he reached it, he hit the clutch, and the engine raced crazily in neutral.

Four figures swam frantically toward them. Swift Elk reached the command boat first and Falconi hauled him in. Next Paulo arrived followed by Hank Valverde. The last in was Chris Hawkins.

Each of the soaked Black Eagles had arrived swimming with one hand while carrying his M16 in the other. Even in the dizzy confusion of being tossed over upside down, they had each had presence of mind to hang onto their weapons.

Chris made a quick inspection of his crew while the chief re-engaged the clutch and sped toward the Bravo boat.

"All hands right as rain," Chris reported to Falconi. He turned in time to see his boat rise up again to sink stern first into the river. "Oh, damn!" he said, swearing in the subtle manner of upperclass New England. "I've lost my ship."

"We're gonna lose this one if we ain't careful!" Archie yelled. "Look! Here comes the three bastards like bats outta hell!"

"We're getting out of this shit," Falconi said into his radio to Top. "Pull out all stops and make for the south."

Both Black Eagle craft were now headed toward Tam Nuroc at top speed. Fusillades of heavy machine gun rounds whistled and whacked around their heads while the heavy swoosh of flying rockets split the air between and around the vessels.

The windshield in front of Chief Brewster exploded as two 12.7 millimeter slugs smacked into it. Falconi grabbed the microphone of the AN/PRC-41 radio that was situated between himself and the Navy CPO. "Naughty Norski. This is Falcon. Over."

Warrant Officer Stensland's voice crackled out loud and clear. "This is Naughty Norski. We're still hanging back. What's happening, Falcon? Over."

"We're in deep shit. Fly up the river. You'll see what's happening. Out."

Over in the Bravo boat, Blue Richards fought for control as a rocket slammed sideways along the hull. The projectile didn't strike solidly enough to explode, and streaked skyward in an aimless flight.

But for one brief and terrifying moment, it looked like the Bravos would slam full-speed into the river bank, but the plucky Blue was able to guide the craft back out into open water beside the command boat.

Then Top spun on his heel and dropped to the deck. A large crimson stain spread across his tiger

120

fatigues. His face, pasty white, was twisted in agony as he tried to get up.

He'd bumped against Blue when he fell. The Seal knew someone had been hit. "Corpsman!" he yelled.

Malpractice stopped firing and started to crawl toward the wounded sergeant major. But Top gritted his teeth and motioned him to return to his firing position.

Malpractice gave his team leader a visual examination, then reluctantly obeyed the silent order to leave him alone.

Machine gun fire hit the control console and the wheel spun loosely in Blue's hands. "The control cables are hit!" he yelled. Unable to guide the boat now, he grabbed the throttle, determined to keep it going wide-open as long as the vessel was able to travel down river.

Top, in pain, saw the situation. He grabbed the Prick-Six. "Falcon—Bravo—can't steer—shit—get away—"

Falconi, over in the control boat, yelled at the chief. "They've lost steering."

"Oh, Christ!" Chief Brewster shouted. "They've had it, sir!"

Then Blue, unable to steer, had to cut back on the throttles as the launch headed toward the shore.

The commander of the leading NVA craft to the rear correctly assessed the situation and ordered his helmsman to close in on the disabled boat. The enemy machine gun swung toward the Black Eagles kneeling behind the gunwale. It was a target that couldn't be missed.

Then the Naughty Norski swept in at tree-top level.

Gunnar Olson sat in the gunner's cockpit of the Cobra gunship. Located in front, and lower down than the pilot, he had a perfect view of their target.

Both his hands gripped the turret sight as he waited eagerly for a target. "Gimme a more nose-down attitude, Erick."

"You got it, *venn*," Stensland said. He eased the stick forward a bit. "Can you see better now?"

"You bet. There's three boats chasing two," Gunnar the Gunner said.

"How are we lined up on them?" Stensland asked.

Gunnar didn't answer. Instead he hit the buttons for the grenade launcher and sent a pair of 40-millimeter rounds streaking toward the river. Both slammed into the lead boat and stopped it so quickly that the bow dipped deep into the muddy water.

The Naughty Norski streaked past, then banked sharply as Stensland brought her around again. Although he was the pilot, it was Gunnar the Gunner who was in charge now. The young Norwegian-American knew exactly what he wanted. "Take us in low from the front again. I'll give the bastards a dose of the mini-guns."

"Here we go," Stensland said.

This time the Naughty Norski came in so low over the two Black Eagles boats that the occupants instinctively ducked their heads. At the correct moment, Gunnar fired the mini-guns.

The two six-barreled M-134 miniguns, one each mounted inboard on each wing, cut loose with 7.62 millimeter rounds at a wrecking rate of 4,000 rounds per minute.

The water around the two NVA boats sprayed upward, and the bodies of the crewmen hurled to the deck gave stark evidence of Gunnar's accuracy. Once again the Naughty Norski streaked upward.

Back on the river, Falconi hit the transmit button on the AN/PRC-41. "Norski, this is Falcon. The enemy pursuit has ceased. Over."

"Roger, Falcon," radioed back Stensland. "We can go back in and finish off the bastards. Over."

"Negative, Norski. Check the other side of Tam Nuroc for enemy activity. We don't want to get overrun while you're to the north. I think the bastards are spread up and down the Song Cai. Over."

"Wilco," Stensland acknowledged. "I'll raise you after a quick recon. Out."

Their retreat now over, the two Black Eagle vessels slowed down. Malpractice McCorckel could now give Top Gordon his full attention. The sergeant major, ashen-faced but game, gave the medic a quick assessment. "It didn't—come out—down deep."

Malpractice listened for the wheezing of a lung wound, but could detect none. He checked the injury carefully, noting that Top had taken a heavy hit in the upper chest. If the round had been an inch higher, it would have torn a hunk out of the sergeant major's heart. "It ain't too bad, Top," Malpractice lied, stuffing a field-dressing into the bloody mess. "I'll clean you up and we'll get you hauled out of here."

Top grimaced and nodded. The initial numbness was beginning to wear off. Calvin Culpepper squatted down and laid a hand on the team leader's shoulder. "You'll be back in Tokyo before you know it, Top. Prob'ly have more trouble with hard-ons than anything else."

Top smiled as best he could. "I'll just keep it hid from them nurses."

"Yeah!" Calvin said with a grin. "They ain't got no morals, 'specially with a goodlookin' ol' dude like you."

Top forced himself to keep smiling. "If that fucking Archie can get one, I can get a dozen."

"Damn straight, Top!" Calvin agreed.

At the same time Malpractice had finished his

temporary first aid, the command boat pulled alongside. Chief Brewster tossed a line to Blue. "We'll tow you on into Tam Nuroc."

"Roger that!" Blue said catching the rope. He immediately began the task of attaching it to the bow.

Malpractice stood up. "Top's been hit, sir. He's down on the deck. I don't know how bad he is except he's conscious and talking."

Falconi, over in the command boat, sighed audibly. The last thing he needed was to have a good combat leader like Top Gordon taken out of the fight. But any further thoughts on the dilemma were interrupted by Chief Warrant Officer Stensland's voice over the radio.

"Falcon, this is Norski. Bad news. There's NVA both north and south of you. Over."

"Roger, I expected that," Falconi replied. "Which is the weakest concentration? Over."

"To the south. The camp to the north is a large one and located on a big, looping bend in the river. Over."

"Roger, Norski. We're done for the day. You can return to base. Over."

"Roger. Do you want us to arrange to have you pulled out of there? There's enough H34s at Dak Bla to do the job. Over."

"Negative! Negative! Out!" Falconi was pissed off. "What we need are some heavier weapons, not a goddamned flight out of the war."

"I agree, sir," the chief said, handling the wheel. He eased forward on the throttle until the line between the two craft was taut. Then he increased speed to begin the trip back to the village. "But what can we do until the paperwork mill shits us some?"

"We can go south and make a requisition on our own," Falconi said.

"South? Excuse me, sir, but that's where Stensland

124

said there was more NVA."

"Don't think of them as our enemy," Falconi said. "Think of them as a belligerent supply depot." He turned to Hank Valverde. "What kind of scuba gear did we get?"

"We got a couple of Emerson closed-circuit sets, sir," Hank answered.

Falconi was pleasantly surprised for a change. "Emersons? Are you sure of that?"

"Yes, sir," Hank said. "I took 'em outta the packs and checked the stuff out myself."

Archie Dobbs glanced over at Falconi. "That's the kind that don't show bubbles," he needlessly informed him. "They're real good for sneaky swimming."

"Good," Falconi said leaning against the console. "That'll make it a lot easier for you and Blue when you swim into that NVA post down south."

"Oh, shit!" Archie said.

"Oh, shit indeed!" Falconi replied.

CHAPTER 12

The villagers of Tam Nuroc were in a jittery mood now.

The people gathered in nervous groups, chattering among themselves, obviously alarmed at what they had so clearly noted: the Americans had left with three boats and returned with two — and one of which was towed. They could see the considerable combat damage to the surviving craft, and duly noted the badly wounded man carried into the large hut used as a dispensary during infrequent visits by government doctors and nurses.

If it hadn't been for the helicopter gunship that had made a couple of appearances that day, there would have been wholesale panic.

There was enough uneasiness for the local militia to be put on a readiness status and the commander, an army veteran named Trang, called on Lieutenant Colonel Falconi.

Falconi greeted him politely, even using the rank of captain in referring to him. *"Chao ong, Dai-Uy."*

"*Chao ong, Trung-Ta,*" Trang said saluting in the French fashion. "I wish to inform you that I have put my men on special alert."

"*Cam on ong,*" Falconi thanked him. "We appreciate the support."

Trang spoke with the natural diplomacy so well practiced in the Far East. He did this by not coming directly to the point right away nor voicing any fears or uncertainties that he felt. Instead, he judiciously opened his concerned inquiries with a quiet understatement. "I see that you have been out on a mission."

Falconi knew what the man was leading up to. He played the Oriental social game with him. "Yes. My men and I sought out the enemy."

"Ah! Did you find any?"

Falconi almost laughed aloud. Top was being tended in the dispensary, they were short one boat, and the other two were shot to shit—and that included one that was not even running. But the lieutenant colonel controlled himself. "*Chac-chan.* We fought a small battle."

"I see," Trang said. He took a deep breath. "Were you victorious?"

"Our *may bay truc-thang*—the helicopter—attacked the enemy and drove them off."

"*Murn ong!*" Trang exclaimed. He paused again. "Do you think the enemy will now come here?"

Falconi shook his head. "I doubt it, *Dai-Uy* Trang. But it is a good idea to keep the milita on alert."

"I will do so, of course," Trang said.

Falconi appreciated the other man's concern. He would like to have given him more information, but the American could not afford to put any trust in the Vietnamese other than allow him and his men to remain armed. "Please keep me informed as to the local situation," he asked.

"Of course." Trang saluted. *Chao ong, Trung-Ta.*

"*Chao ong, Dai-Uy,*" Falconi said. He watched the man leave the hut, then turned to Swift Elk. "Will the men be ready for another mission in about three or four hours?"

Swift Elk, now the acting senior non-commissioned officer, checked his watch. "Yes, sir." He glanced meaningfully at Falconi. "I noticed you didn't say anything to Trang about us going out again."

"I don't trust anybody but us in this situation," Falconi said. "Except for a couple of folks that I have no choice about."

"That would be Choy and the whorehouse lady, right?"

"Right," Falconi said. "Let's check on Top, then make sure that Archie and Blue are getting squared away properly for a scuba mission."

"Yes, sir," Swift Elk said, following his commander into the next room.

The sun was a red disk floating over the tallest trees when the Black Eagles left Tam Nuroc for the second time that day.

The lead boat was manned by the Bravos, reinforced with Falconi, Chris Hawkins and Paulo Garcia. The rear boat, with its steering gear quickly but expertly repaired, was piloted by Chief Brewster and carried Swift Elk, Hank Valverde and Calvin Culpepper. Archie Dobbs and Blue Richards also rode along with those stalwarts, but they were completely outfitted in scuba gear and lay out of sight on the cockpit deck. There was also a buoy between them. One of Calvin Culpepper's field-expedient pyrotechnic inventions was attached to the flotation device.

Paulo Garcia kept the throttle at half-speed while Falconi studied the terrain through his binoculars. "Stensland said there was an NVA river camp about five klicks to the south," he said half-aloud.

"That's where the shit's going down?" Paulo asked.

"Right," Falconi answered.

Everyone knew exactly *what* they were going to do—they just didn't know *where* or *when*. Without time tables or a proper map reconnaissance, it was impossible to plan any better. It was the sort of situation that Archie Dobbs described as "like going into a dark, strange bar with the idea of kicking everybody's ass in the place—there is a hell of a good potential for a nasty surprise."

Another hour passed and darkness was threatening to descend over them when contact was finally made. A mammoth *song* tree leaned well out over the water, blocking the view of the west bank. When the Bravo boat eased past this natural cover, the occupants found themselves less than fifty meters from an NVA patrol boat.

The enemy crew—just as surprised—were eating their evening rice. Nobody reacted for a split second, until Falconi slapped Paulo's shoulder. "Spin and git!" He had been holding onto the Prick-six and yelled into it. "Action! Action!"

Back on the command boat, Archie and Blue grabbed the buoy and flung it overboard. They dove into the water behind it, and Archie reached up to the device attached to it and pulled the lanyard. Immediately a hissing, boiling cloud of thick smoke roared out and quickly spread.

Then he and Blue sucked on their mouthpieces and dove deep for the silty bottom of the Song Cai.

Chief Brewster, at the wheel, waited for the Bravo

boat to streak past him, then he fired up the engine of his own vessel to full speed and turned about. The smoke pot continued to emit its thick cloud as the command boat towed it in pursuit of the Bravo's launch.

The NVA crew, taking a full three minutes to get aboard and rev up their own boat, roared out into the river in time to see the blinding smoke obscuring all vision and foiling any chance of pursuit.

The senior man, a veteran sergeant, spat into the water. "Cowards!" he said contemptuously. "They are afraid to fight."

One of the riflemen impetuously fired a short burst from his AK47 at the fleeing Americans.

"*Durng lai!*" the sergeant scolded. "Do not waste the people's ammunition." He motioned to the helmsman. "Take us back. Those *cho* haven't the stomach to face us."

The Red boat, in reverse, eased back toward its anchorage. A few meters away, coming to the surface to look around, Archie Dobbs oriented himself. Then he went back into the invisible world of the muddy under-river and tapped Blue Richards on the shoulder. The two, swimming slowly and deep, headed toward the enemy camp.

Chuck Fagin studied the five cards in his hand under the dim light of the 40-watt bulb. He held a respectable hand of two pair—jacks and eights. He took a drag on his cigar and stared across the table to study the back of his opponents' cards. Things looked good to him on his own personal marked deck they were using until he noted that the colonel across from him had three of a kind.

"I fold," Fagin said. He turned his cards down on

the table. "Who dealt this shit?"

"Me," the colonel said, smiling. The others at the table had seen his raise. They waited impatiently for him to show his cards. "Three of a kind," he announced exposing the hand for all to view.

The others, a major and a captain, moaned aloud as the pot was raked in.

The card players sat in a side room off Fagin's main office. It was late as the air-conditioner hummed over the sound of rippling cards and clinking poker chips. Fagin, complaining of a headache, wore dark glasses as he took the deck from the previous dealer for his turn at the chore.

"Seven-toed Pete," he announced passing out the cards for his favorite game of stud. "Nothing wild."

The deck was a special CIA device, and Fagin could read the marks on it by using the dark glasses that allowed him to see the faintest coding on the backs. He knew, from hand-to-hand, what each of his opponents held. To keep them from becoming suspicious, he had been losing at a steady pace. He'd also been liberal with his scotch and bourbon, and his guests were getting close to happy intoxication.

By the time all the cards were dealt, the colonel had a pair of tens showing, but Fagin could see that there was another in his hole cards. The lucky sonofabitch had been rolling through the evening's play with three of a kind and full houses every third or fourth hand. The pile of chips in front of him was impressive.

Fagin had a pair of sevens showing—and two more in the hole. Now was the time to reel the sucker in. "What's the pair of tens bet?"

The colonel smiled drunkenly and shoved out a twenty dollar chip.

"I call," said the captain.

"Fuck it," the major said announcing his with-

131

drawal from the hand.

"I'll see that and raise you twenty," Fagin said.

The colonel laughed. "Bluffing a bluffer, Fagin? No goddamned way. I'll see that raise—" He shoved out another chip. "And go up another'n." He leered at the captain. "Forty bucks to you."

"Shit."

"The limit is one more raise," Fagin said. He saw the colonel's bet and went another twenty.

"I'm in, asshole," the colonel said staying in the game. "Whattaya got?"

"Four sevens," Fagin said.

"You ain't getting lucky finally, are you?" the colonel said who could easily afford the loss.

"Could be," Fagin said grinning. "Whose deal?"

The NVA camp fire had all but died out.

A guard walked listlessly on the river bank near their boat while his comrades settled down for the night. Their quiet murmuring went on for another half hour before the NVA troopers drifted off to sleep.

Two figures slowly emerged from the muddy waters on the far side of the boat. Archie Dobbs took his mouthpiece out and sucked in natural air. After so long on the scuba tanks, the fresher variety seemed almost delicious.

Blue Richards did the same. An experienced military diver, he hardly made a ripple as he eased through the water. He waited until Archie reached the bank before he grasped the side of the boat and silently pulled himself aboard.

Archie had taken his flippers off and abandoned them. He needed to move as quietly as possible in the shadows near the clearing where the Reds had established their camp. He watched the guard's circuit several times before picking a vantage point at the edge of the jungle.

The sentry, feeling sleepy, shuffled along with his head down. He was anxious to be relieved so that he could settle down in his mosquito netting to sleep the rest of the night away. Unknown to him, he'd just stepped past a soldier who was an enemy to him, his cause and his nation.

Archie moved fast.

One hand clamped over the guard's mouth while the other drove the stilleto under the the rib cage and up into the vital organs. A quick twist to ensure massive hemorrhaging, then the blade was pulled out and swung across to slash the jugular vein. This action would speed up the emptying of life's blood.

By the time Archie slowly lowered the cadaver to the sandy ground, he was sticky with the wet liquid. He took another look at the NVA sleeping over by the glowing coals. There was not a stir nor murmur. Archie moved to the boat.

Blue hardly gave his friend time to swing on board before he punched the starter. The motor whirred and died.

The sleeping men stirred.

Blue tried again and failed.

The Red soldiers, shouting and cursing, were now on their feet. Fully awake, they had all grabbed their AK-47s.

Archie leaped up on the foredeck and spun the Soviet heavy machine gun around. He instinctively ducked as the first spattering of rounds zipped around him.

Blue got the engine going and poured on the throttle. Archie cranked the cocking handle and cut loose with a long fire burst that hosed tracers into the group of NVA. The front two staggered under the impact of the rounds and collapsed to the ground.

Archie stopped firing to steady the barrel, then cut loose again as the boat sped out into the water. His final burst dumped another of the Reds, then the boat was out of range.

Archie joined Blue behind the control console. "Be careful in this fucking dark!" he yelled. "We'll run aground!"

"Find a spotlight or something," Blue hollered back.

Archie fumbled around until he felt a cold metal dish-like object. He finally found a pistol-grip device and located a switch on it. "I got the mother!"

"All right!" Blue yelled as a cone of light exploded outward showing at least twenty meters of the river to their front. "Next stop Tam Nuroc." He grinned at Archie. "We done good, huh?"

Archie patted the heavy machine gun and noted the rocket tubes on both port and starboard sides. "Yeah, Blue. As a matter of fact, we done *damned* good!"

You are the luckiest sonofabitch!"

Fagin looked at the colonel. "I gotta admit that everything seemed to be going my way for the past coupla hours."

The colonel sighed. The major and captain had already left dead broke. "Will you take a check?"

Fagin lit a fresh cigar. "That's a lot o' money—two thousand smackaroonies."

"Hey!" the colonel exclaimed. "The check is good, all right? Do you think I'm crazy enough to give you a bum—"

"You're the American S-4 rep for that Philippine artillery battalion, aren't you?"

"Sure," the colonel said. "Also for one of the Thai outfits too." He laughed bitterly. "Why are you asking, Fagin? Do you want a 105 howitzer or something?"

"How about a couple of quad-fifties?"

The colonel leaped to his feet. "Are you crazy? I could go to jail for—"

"Relax," Fagin said soothingly pouring the man another bourbon. "Would you go to jail if you sent 'em through channels to a SOG detachment?"

The colonel sat down. "Naw, but it would be irregular as hell." The suspicion he felt was clear in the inquisitive expression on his face. "Why don't you use SOG ordnance—Major Kelsey would be the man."

"That sonofabitch Kelsey won't give me any weaponry," Fagin explained. "He says we're under the 5th Group because the guys are billeted out at Nui Dep now."

"So see the 5th's S-4."

"They can't support us, and you have some surplus arms for replacements," Fagin said. "Hell, they're anti-aircraft weapons. The VC don't have an air force. Them Filippinos and Thais don't have any use for quad-fifties."

"Nobody wants these particular weapons," the colonel admitted. "They're really just collecting dust and rust." He sipped the drink and waited for Fagin to continue.

"I've tried your command once already," Fagin said. "They turned me down for no damned good reason."

"That's because they work for me," the colonel said, "and my motto has always been 'Always say no unless there's a helluva good reason to say yes'."

"Would it be a good enough reason if I called off

your poker debt to me?" Fagin asked.

The colonel took another slug of whiskey. "Where do you want 'em sent?"

Fagin grinned. "I have this pal named Falconi—"

CHAPTER 13

The mechanic considered himself a couple of steps above his fellow soldiers despite the fact he was a loyal, practicing communist who believed in a class-less society. But, after all, there were some people who had skills and talents that lifted them above the common herd.

His comrades, to be sure, were true and steadfast Marxists who faithfully served the cause of advancing world socialism with as much fervor as he, but the mechanic not only did all this too, but he had that valuable skill and trade which had taken so many months of training and schooling to acquire.

He was a welder.

The sparks from his torch flew out in bright splatters as he put the finishing touches on the bar he'd mounted amidships on the patrol boat. He flipped his mask up and inspected the work with his naked eyes, then turned toward his commanding officer. "I have finished, Comrade Captain."

Ngy sat on the gunwale where he'd been waiting for

the task to be completed. He stood up and walked the few steps necessary to check the handiwork. Satisfied it was well done, he snapped his fingers. *"Sung may!"*

The two soldiers who had been standing off to one side of the deck, picked up the Soviet DShK heavy machine gun and staggered up to the newly constructed frame. After manhandling the weighty weapon up into position, they slipped the pivot into the mounting hole and twisted the locking lever shut.

Ngy stepped up and grabbed the weapon's handles. He pulled and pushed with all his strength until he was satisfied the weld job was strong and permanent. *"Tot!"* he said in mild praise. "This will do splendidly."

The mechanic smiled proudly. He reached out and patted his own handiwork with the same affection he might have shown a son. "Thank you, Comrade Captain!"

Ngy smiled and patted the machine gun. "One advantage of the DShK is that it is also an anti-aircraft weapon as well as a tactical arm."

"Of course, Comrade Captain," the mechanic said.

"You will prepare the other four boats in this same manner, Comrade," Ngy ordered. "And each will be as carefully inspected as this one," Ngy warned him.

"Do not worry, Comrade Captain," the man said with a salute. "My welds are as strong as the tenets of Chairman Ho." Then he added more modestly, "but even they will not last as long." The mechanic quickly gathered up his tools with the help of the other two soldiers and hurried off the launch to attend the other craft.

They almost bumped into the eager adjutant who had taken a shaky walk across the floating dock. "Comrade Captain Ngy!" he called out. "You have a visitor."

Ngy was mildly irritated. "Who is it?" he asked testily.

"It is Comrade Tho May."

"I am on my way," Ngy said. "Please inform him." Any time this spy appeared, it was of the utmost importance for Ngy to quickly report to him.

Tho May, dressed as a peasant, had helped himself to one of Ngy's cigarettes that were kept in a box on the office desk. He looked up at Ngy's entrance. "Greetings, Comrade."

"Greetings to you, Comrade," Ngy said anxiously. "Do you bring news?"

"Yes," Tho May said. He pointed out toward the dock through the open window. "I notice you are installing anti-aircraft weapons."

Ngy nodded. "*Dung*. We were badly mauled by a helicopter in our last meeting with the Americans."

"It seems you have a surprise in store for them in regards to those machine guns," Tho May said dryly.

Again Ngy bobbed his head in an affirmative manner. "Once we have shot down their air cover, we will be able to destroy them almost at our leisure. They are but lightly armed."

"They are now in possession of a heavy machine gun and two rocket launchers," Tho May said.

"Damn!" Ngy exclaimed through clenched teeth. "I had hoped their supply service would be slower than that."

"They did not get these weapons through their ordnance branch," Tho May said after a deep drag off the cigarette. "They have stolen a patrol boat from your unit."

"From the reconnaissance launch operating in the south?" Ngy asked.

"The same, Comrade."

"Those idiots! They had orders to stay well away

139

from Tam Nuroc," Ngy said angrily.

"They did not go to Tam Nuroc," Tho May informed him. "The Americans went after them. Two of the gangsters in underwater devices sneaked into the camp at night. After killing the man on guard duty, they took the boat."

Ngy walked over to the desk and treated himself to one of his own cigarettes. He felt a twinge of nervousness at this particular bit of intelligence. An enemy who can perform such bold deeds is not to be taken lightly.

Tho May sat down in a wicker chair by the wall. "I also now know the identity of the unit you face."

Ngy's eyes widened with curiosity. "Yes, Comrade?"

"They are called the Black Eagles and are commanded by a lieutenant colonel named Falconi," Tho May said. "Does that mean anything to you?"

Ngy shook his head. "I have not heard of them."

Tho was not surprised. The North Vietnamese Army did not readily keep its personnel enlightened as to certain aspects of the war that were deemed unpleasant to the communist side. "They are an elite unit made up of many branches of the imperialist services. You will not be surprised to learn that in the past, they have done much harm to our cause. If you were to destroy them, you would be recognized as a true hero of Marxism."

"Are you sure they have but the one boat that is fully armed?" Ngy asked.

"I am positive, Comrade," Tho May said.

"I have four such craft, and I can call down several more if needed," Ngy said. "So, even with the ones on hand, I can still be certain of destroying the helicopter, then going full bore after the other launches."

"I advise you to waste no time, Comrade," Tho

May said. This statement was not so much advice as it was an open threat to the captain.

"Don't worry," Ngy said taking the ominous hint. "Excuse me while I set the wheels of vengeance and victory into immediate operation." He abruptly turned and went back outside yelling for his adjutant.

The officer, who had been watching the welding project being performed on the boats, jumped around as if he'd heard a shot. He rushed back to report to his commander. "Yes, Comrade Captain?"

"Put the men on alert," Ngy said. "As soon as the work on the boats is finished we are going to attack the Americans at Tam Nuroc."

"The men have been on a ready status for the past two days, Comrade Captain," the adjutant said proudly. "They can be ready to load their boats and go into action in less than a half hour."

Ngy smiled despite himself. He could already feel the weight of newly won medals pinned to his tunic.

Lieutenant Colonel Falconi turned the lantern down until the hut was lit by only a dull, yellow glow. He walked over to the table and chair that served as his desk. After lighting a cigarette, he sat down and looked at the man across the room from him.

Ray Swift Elk relaxed on a wooden stool and leaned back against a support post. He'd just posted the guard and inspected the militia sentries with Trang. A caffeine addict, he sipped at a cup of hot C-ration coffee.

"Are we secure for the night?" Falconi asked stretching his feet out.

"Yeah," Swift Elk said without much enthusiasm. "If the militia can be trusted. If not, and we're hit, then I'd say the boys could inflict a lot of damage

141

before—"

Falconi looked at him. "Go on."

Swift Elk sighed. "—before we get overrun."

They lapsed into thoughtful silence, both staring at the floor until Malpractice McCorckel came into the hut. The medic took a chair near Falconi. "Top's having a rough time," Malpractice said.

"Okay," Falconi acknowledged. "We can get him medevaced any time you say."

But Malpractice shook his head. "No can do, Skipper. He ain't bleeding right now, but there's a slug in his chest that could tear into the aorta."

"What's that?" Swift Elk asked.

"It's the main artery that carries blood from the left ventricle of the heart," Malpractice explained. "If that baby goes, there's nothing can be done to stop the hemorrhaging in time."

"Then what do we do?" Falconi asked.

"We can only wait and see if his life signs stabilize," Malpractice said. "His pulse is so damned weak and erratic, I'm not sure of his true condition. If he goes into shock, we've lost him for sure."

Falconi stuck his hand into his jacket and wiped at the clammy sweat that covered his chest. "Shit."

"At least I found some help," Malpractice said. "I can get some sleep tonight."

Swift Elk was puzzled. "All the guys are out on guard posts. Who's helping you?"

"One of the local girls—name of Xinh—she ain't a nurse, but she's had some first aid training," Malpractice said. "She's been to the Catholic girls school in Nha Trang, so she speaks French and English pretty good."

Ray Swift Elk was ever the intelligence sergeant. "Can you trust her, Malpractice?"

"Hell, Injun, I *got* to," Malpractice said. He was

142

silent for several moments. "Damn, I get sick o' the guys getting hurt and killed." He looked up at Falconi. "Remember Jack Galchaser? Dinky Dow? Lightfingers O'Quinn?"

"Yeah," Falconi said softly. "I remember 'em."

"Ol' Lightfingers was a damned good supply man," Malpractice said.

"We got Hank Valverde now," Swift Elk said.

Malpractice's face reddened with anger. "Well he ain't as good as Lightfingers, see?"

Swift Elk rubbed his hand across his mouth. "I suppose not," he said in a calming tone.

"Poor fuckers are dead," Malpractice said, getting up. "The poor dead guys." He walked to the door and stopped to speak without turning around. "I got to save Top." He left the hut and walked across the narrow village street to the thatched building that served as the village dispensary. At that particular time, it was a hospital for only a single patient. When Malpractice stepped into the room, he saw Xinh gently wiping Top's brow.

The girl smiled at the American. "He sweat a little, Malcomb."

Malpractice knelt down and put a hand on Top's forehead. "He seems a little cooler too. I'll take his temperature after a while." He took his wounded friend's pulse. "Not good. Still fluttery."

"We need a doctor," Xinh said.

"One would certainly come in handy, that's for sure. But there's not much we can do about that." Malpractice yawned with fatigue. "Maybe I'll get some sleep."

"Yes, Malcomb," Xinh said. "I watch Top some more while you rest."

"Thanks," Malpractice said. "You've really been a lot of help, Xinh. Really."

She smiled shyly and lowered her eyes. "I am pleased if my humble efforts ease your burden, Malcomb."

"They sure do," the medic said. "There's no doubt on that score." He went over to the sleeping mat in the corner and lay down. He treated himself to a leisurely look at Xinh.

She was a pretty girl, nineteen years old, with long, shiny black hair. Shapely, with small but firm uplifted breasts, Malpractice McCorckel would have lusted after her like a stud bull if he hadn't been so damnably, terribly tired. Also, and most importantly, he was also worried sick about Top. So instead of feeling strong sexual desires to possess the girl, he had tender emotions and genuine affection.

Damn! he thought to himself, it's been a helluva long time since I was friends with a broad with no real thoughts of screwing her.

With that noble thought, he closed his eyes and drifted off into a troubled sleep.

Fleurette Hue bowed her formal farewells to the departing NVA officer. His men had been treated to a hasty visit with her girls that had caused a flurry of mercenary sexual activity at the whorehouse.

The soldiers practically stormed the place since they'd been given so little time. This was most unusual. In the past, when it was a certain unit's turn to enjoy the pleasures offered by the girls, they had all night or at least several long hours to pursue the satisfaction of their lusts. This time there was but some hasty coupling that left a couple of the house inmates a bit bruised and upset.

Fleurette waited until the patrol boat's engine was fired up and it pulled back into the river before she waved her final farewell and returned inside. The girls were gathered in the sitting room for their evening meal which had been interrupted by the unexpected onslaught.

"They were very rude!" one of the whores said angrily as she squatted down by the table. "I have a bruise on my leg."

"They didn't even take off their pants all the way," another complained. "My stomach is all scratched from belt buckles."

Fleurette clucked in sympathy while the maid spooned bowlfuls of fish soup for her and the women. "Why do you think they acted like that? What was their rush?"

The girl with the sore leg scowled. "It was their turn to come here. But they are going to war so their commander didn't give them as much time as usual. So they all had to fuck us fast to give every soldier a turn."

Fleurette slowly sipped her soup. "I thought they were already at war."

"They go to fight a special battle," one of the whores said as she tenderly inspected a bruised breast. "They bragged about it."

"Yes!" several chorused.

Another girl piped up. "They have put on special guns to shoot down flying machines."

From that point on the conversation died out as the tired prostitutes finished their meal so they could withdraw to repair themselves from the semi-rapes they had endured.

Fleurette went back to her room. She would never cease to be amazed by the psychological side of males in which they looked down on prostitutes, but would brag of their exploits in order to impress such fallen women. The madame took a piece of paper and the old fashioned pen she used to write with, and dipped it in the ink bottle on her desk. Then she laboriously wrote:

Les soldats communistes ont mitrailleuse sur leur bateaux pour tirer avions.

Then she folded it into a tiny square and left the house to go down to the river where the big tree leaned out over the water.

Master Sergeant Swift Elk walked softly up the village street, instinctively sticking to the shadows as he held his M16 at the ready.

He'd just completed a check on the Black Eagle sentries and was satisfied that they were well placed and alert. He didn't bother with the local militia. As amateur soldiers, he feared they might become startled if he approached their posts—especially if they'd momentarily dozed off—and he didn't want to chance getting shot by some startled or nervous civilian-soldier.

He stepped through the poncho blanket curtain rigged across the hut and joined Lieutenant Colonel Falconi in the hot, muggy interior of the headquarters hut.

Falconi, lying still to keep as cool as possible, barely turned his head at the Sioux Indian's entrance. "How's it look out there, Ray?" he asked.

"Everything's copasetic," Swift Elk replied. He went to the lister bag strung up on a long rope from the rafters and filled his canteen cup at its spigot. "I looked in on Top before making the rounds."

"I just got back from there fifteen minutes ago," Falconi said. "He seems mighty weak."

146

"Yeah," Swift Elk said squatting down to slowly sip the tepid water. "But at least Malpractice has some help from that girl Xinh."

Falconi was thoughtful for several moments. "I'm worried about him."

"Malpractice can get him well enough for a medevac," Swift Elk said. "Don't worry."

"I don't mean Top," Falconi said flatly.

"Yeah," Swift Elk said. "I know what's on your mind. Ol' Malpractice is showing some signs of—" He hesitated.

"In civilian life they'd politely call it exhaustion, or at worst, a nervous breakdown," Falconi said.

"Let's face up to it," Swift Elk said, "what we have developing here is a classic case of combat fatigue. Too many guys have died and been hurt. It's tearing at Malpractice's soul."

"He's sensitive as hell," Falconi said. "But I suppose that's what made him work so damned hard to get awarded a medic's MOS in the first place."

"All we can do is keep an eye on him," Swift Elk said. He sighed aloud. "If he goes around the bend, his days as a Black Eagle are over."

"You're the top kick of this outfit now," Falconi said. "I'm going to have to rely on you to keep me up to speed on the situation."

"Yessir."

"Hell of a thing being a soldier," Falconi remarked.

Swift Elk displayed a lopsided grin. "Yeah. Especially when you have to be a human being at the same time."

Falconi nodded. He was silent for a few moments more, then closed his eyes. Swift Elk watched him drift off to sleep, then stood up and tip-toed across the room in his jungle boots. He turned the lantern down, and the hut became dark. He went over to his air mattress and slipped under the mosquito netting to lie down on it. After a few moments he sat up to remove his boots and uniform before settling back in the heat to sleep in his underwear.

Out in the jungle, grasping their weapons, the Black Eagles on guard passed their watches as the long, slow tropical night dragged by.

CHAPTER 14

Chuck Fagin, clad in a khaki safari suit, displayed his ID to the guard at the main gate of Tan Son Nhut's Military Air Transport terminal, then drove his jeep onto the base.

He traveled slowly and deliberately, displaying a perfect example of the careful driver. He made all proper hand signals, obeyed traffic signs to the letter and displayed great courtesy to pedestrians. Fagin continued on toward the operations office situated between the hangars where the largest planes used by the U.S. Air Force — C-123s, C-130s and C-143s — were housed and serviced.

When he arrived at his destination, he discreetly parked in the area marked for visitors. Usually, in his brash style, he took any goddamned parking place he wanted, but Fagin was on his best behavior that particular day. This was not from any change in his personality. The CIA officer simply didn't want to attract any unpleasant or unnecessary attention to himself.

Everything about him could be classified in one word: *unauthorized*.

The mission he was on was *unauthorized*. The materials he was dealing with were *unauthorized*. And, finally, his plan for disposing of this equipment was *unauthorized*.

Fagin walked over to the office complex and again politely displayed his ID. This time it was for a husky young air policeman standing by the entrance. The AP, however, was a bit brusque. "Who is it you wanna see, Mister—" He looked at the card again. "—Mister Fagin?"

Fagin smiled through clenched teeth. "The operations officer, son."

The AP grinned back. "I can't let you in unless you give me a name."

"A name?"

"Yeah. I gotta know who it is you wanna see."

"You mean the particular individual?" Fagin asked hiding his nervousness.

Continuing to smile, the AP nodded his head. "That's right."

Fagin's eyes quickly swept the parking places in front of the building. He couldn't see them all, but he did note one marked for a Captain Tetley. He laughed and looked back at the AP. "I guess I'm getting old, son. Just can't remember names like I used to. The guy I need to see is named Tetley."

"Tetley?" the AP remarked. "Mister, he ain't the operations officer."

"Did I say operations officer?" Fagin asked. "I meant I had to see Tetley." He continued to speak rapidly. "This is the right place isn't it?" He adopted a quizzical expression. "Jesus, I hope this is the right place—MATS?"

"Sure, this is MATS," the AP said. "Cap'n Tetley's

150

office is inside." He opened the door and stood back.

"Thank you kindly, son. I appreciate your kindness." He walked down the hall of offices, then paused and glanced back. The AP, scowling suspiciously, was peering at him through the window. Fagin went to the door marked CAPTAIN TETLEY, and boldly knocked.

"Come in."

Fagin walked into the office. "I'm looking for the operations officer."

The Air Force captain behind the desk was mildly irritated. "Well, you're in the wrong place. Go on down the hall to the other side of the building."

"The other side of the building?"

"The other side of the building."

Fagin knew that the AP would be suspicious if he left the office too quickly. "Say, Captain, er, Tetley. Would you mind taking me there?"

"Who the hell are you?" Tetley asked.

Fagin produced his ID. "Fagin — CIA."

"I'm pretty busy, Mister Fagin. It's easy to find. Trust me. All you have to do is walk down the hall outside the door. It'll lead you to the other side of the building where the operations officer is located."

"Please. I'd appreciate an escort. I suppose I'm just security conscious. I'm probably acting like a little old lady, but I don't think folks should be allowed to simply traipse around where they want to in these installations."

The Air Force officer started to make a wisecrack, then gave it up as a serious thought flashed in his mind. There was a good chance that this was a security check of some kind. "Sure. When I saw that CIA ID I figured you'd been here before. You can

151

really believe we're on our toes security-wise around here. Come on with me." He got up and walked around the desk motioning Fagin to follow.

Fagin went out of the office and looked back at the door. The AP was still there. The CIA officer waved at him and nodded, then followed Tetley across the building to a larger office marked OPERATIONS OFFICER.

"Thank you," Fagin said to his departing escort. He turned to the sergeant seated at a desk beside the door leading to an inner room. "Captain Tetley has brought me here to see the operations officer."

"Name, sir?"

"Fagin—Charles Fagin—CIA." He displayed the card once again.

Within ten minutes, Fagin was deeply involved in conversation with the duty operations officer, a harried major named Carney. The main thrust of the talk involved getting an airplane to fly from Tan Son Nhut to Chu Lai.

"No sweat," Carney said. "It won't be difficult getting a seat for you. We have regular flights there all the time."

"My mission is a bit more than a regular flight can handle," Fagin said gently. "I'll also need more than a seat. You see there's some cargo involved."

"What kind of cargo?" Carney asked suspiciously.

"Well . . . two quad-fifties—"

"Goddamnit!"

"And a refrigerator," Fagin quickly added.

"Goddamnit all to hell! A refrigerator? What kind of—"

Fagin settled down on a chair opposite him and lit a cigar to settle in for some hardline persuading.

152

"Have you heard of the Black Eagles?"

"No."

"What about Lt. Col. Winston Baldwin of the United States Air Force?" Fagin asked.

"No."

"Then let me enlighten you," Fagin said. He launched into the story of the Black Eagles' mission that was officially known as Operation Mekong Massacre. It consisted of a raid on the North Vietnamese prison camp that resulted in the rescue of Baldwin from the clutches of a maniacal North Korean brainwashing expert. Fagin elaborated the danger of bringing the sick flyboy through trackless jungle with no less than an entire battalion of NVA hot on their asses. He was particularly descriptive of the final battle on the Song Bo River where the detachment's top sergeant was killed.

When he'd finished, Fagin paused.

"Jesus!" Carney said.

Fagin wasted no time in continuing. He brought the Air Force officer up to date on the present mission — without compromising any classified intelligence — and ended it with a strong emphasis on the fact that the Black Eagles were undermanned and underarmed in a dangerous undertaking.

"The two quad-fifties would be just about right in making things even out in the operation," Fagin emphasized. "There is also a great necessity of not wasting time."

"Jesus!" Carney said again.

"The U.S.A.F. owes Falconi and his boys," Fagin said.

Carney didn't hesitate. "Which do you want? A C-130 or a C-123?"

Fagin was never one to stint. "A nice, powerful C-130 will do nicely."

Malpractice sat on the chair by Falconi's table. "I'm going to have to make a decision within an hour. Either Top gets medevaced or I operate on him so he can be taken out of here without danger to his life."

"Maybe it would be better to call in a surgeon," Falconi suggested.

"Shit, sir!" Malpractice exclaimed. "If that was possible I'd have already done it. There ain't any surgeons hanging around Vietnam making house calls."

"It was only a suggestion, Malpractice," Falconi said.

"Yeah? Well, it was a pretty fucking stupid one!"

Swift Elk, who had been listening across the room, jumped to his feet. "At ease, McCorckel! That's a lieutenant colonel you're talking to."

Malpractice's face blanched white. "Don't give me any o' that top sergeant bullshit! I been in this fucking outfit longer'n you — by about a half dozen missions, buster!"

Swift Elk charged across the room but Falconi leaped to his feet and got between his two men. "Both you jokers back off!" he yelled in angry frustration. "I'm not having two of my senior NCOs pound the hell out of each other!" After Swift Elk had returned to his place, Falconi looked at the medic. "You're getting out of control," he stated.

"I got a job to do," Malpractice said. "I patch up dumb fuckers that get holes blown in 'em. Sometimes I even bury 'em. Hell, I do that more'n anything else.

So far I've had thirty-three—"

"I make out the after-action reports!" Falconi shouted. "I know how many of our people have bought the farm."

"Yes, *sir*!" Malpractice said leaping to his feet and assuming the position of attention. "Permission to withdraw to my patient, *sir*!"

"Get outta here," Falconi hissed.

"Yes, *sir*!" Malpractice saluted and made an about-face, then marched out of the hut.

Swift Elk watched him go. "Maybe all he needs is good ass-kicking."

Falconi shook his head. "He's almost around the bend, the poor fucker."

Archie Dobbs came into the hut. He pointed outside by jerking a thumb over his shoulder. "What the hell's the matter with Malpractice? I said 'hi' to him, and he damned near bit my fucking head off."

"He's in a bad mood," Falconi said.

"Hey, no shit?" Archie said. "By the way, Choy just came in off the river."

"Get him in here," Falconi said. "I want to find out what's going on up north."

"I'm on my way, skipper," Archie said.

Within five minutes Choy had been ushered inside the hut. He was disheveled and exhausted, his clothing badly torn from a long jungle trip. "*Chao ong*, Colonel."

"How are you, Choy?" Falconi asked wearily. "What's the situation with the enemy to the north?"

"How you boys say? S.O.S.—Same Old Shit? Well, that what happening, Colonel. Same Old Shit."

Falconi lit a cigarette. "What about our NVA boat group? Have they been up to anything?"

Choy shook his head. "I go to dead letter drop in tree that hang over the river. There is nothing. So I go and talk with Madame Fleurette. She say that NVA make same patrols like before. Come to visit her girls, then go away."

Ray Swift Elk had been listening from his table across the room. "Was there any indication they had some sort of activity planned for the near future?"

"No. No," Choy said. "The lady say Same Old Shit." He laughed and looked back at Falconi. "Maybe you fellows beat 'em up, eh? They scared for you I think."

Falconi smiled. "Yeah, maybe so. Why don't you rest up a couple of days before you go back?"

"Good idea! *Toi met* — I'm tired. See you later after I eat and take a nice nap. Goodby, Colonel." He waved over at Swift Elk. "Goodby, Injun."

"So long, Choy," Swift Elk said. He waited until the agent left before he spoke. "You sure you want him to stick around, sir? We're going out on ops tomorrow."

"That's exactly why I want him here," Falconi said. "If he's here when we leave, then he can't spill the beans about us — accidentally or otherwise — to any unfriendlies."

"This is a helluva war," Swift Elk said. "Our own informants might be double agents."

Malpractice looked up at Xinh. "You're right. Fluid is collecting in Top's chest." He placed the stethoscope on his patient's heart and listened for a few minutes. "It's a mess in there."

Xinh, her beautiful almond-shaped eyes opened

156

wide in worry, put her hands to her face. "What do we do, Malcomb?"

"I've got to drain the chest cavity and get that bullet out of there," Malpractice said. "I'd hoped we could wait until we could get Top away from Tam Nuroc. But it's been nothing but bad luck lately."

"You can operate? You tell me you're not a doctor," Xinh said.

"I'm a Special Forces medic," Malpractice explained. "That puts me somewhere between a registered nurse and a general practitioner. I've delivered babies, performed appendectomies and sewn up a few ripped bodies to get 'em in shape for a trip to a real hospital. This will be the first time I've gone in deep to pull a slug outta somebody."

"You can do?"

"Baby," Malpractice McCorckel said. "I *gotta* do!"

Xinh watched apprehensively while Malpractice arranged the village dispensary for the necessary medical work. Top's bed was already in an ideal place. Located in the center of the building, it was not near areas where dust or other foreign particles could be whisked over him by gusts or breezes. The medic set up the small operating table and placed his instruments on a stand next to it.

"We're gonna wash our hands with this surgical soap," Malpractice said.

Xinh smiled weakly. "You mean you want me to help?"

"I need you," Malpractice said as a simple statement.

The beautiful Vietnamese girl smiled at him. "Then I help you, Malcomb."

After scrubbing up as best as possible under the

circumstances and donning rubber gloves and surgical masks, the pair began their lifesaving task.

As instructed, Xinh held the wire-framed cup stuffed with cotton over Top's face with one of her small hands. With the other she carefully followed Malpractice's instructions in allowing ether to drip on the device from the bottle she held with the other hand.

Malpractice swabbed Top's chest with iodine. Then he carefully monitored the sergeant major's vital signs. After several moments he picked up the scalpel. He glanced at Xinh.

"Ready?"

"Yes, Malcomb."

"This ain't gonna be pretty," he warned her.

Xinh swallowed hard. "I still want to help you, Malcomb."

The cut was expertly and deeply done. Operating a small manual suction bulb, Malpractice kept the blood clear of the work area. He could see Top's beating heart as the fluid was drawn off. "Now comes the tricky part."

"You are wonderful, Malcomb!"

Malpractice smiled despite himself. "You're exactly what a man needs, Jean."

"Jean?"

"Yeah," he said reaching for the forceps. "That's a female name in English. Sounds a lot like your Vietnamese 'Xinh'. Do you mind if I call you that?"

The girl smiled. "I like the sound. It is almost French."

"Almost," Malpractice said. He'd already spotted the location of the slug that had slammed into Top's chest. He deftly and gently inserted the forceps into

158

the incision, holding them slightly open. Then he closed the instrument and slowly slid it out. The jagged hunk of Russian bullet glistened wetly in the light. "Now we'll insert a surgical drain and really get rid of all that stuff that's been pressing up against Top's heart," Malpractice said. "Then we'll sew him up and get him the hell outta here."

Jean smiled under her mask, then turned her attention to keeping the ether dripping properly onto the cotton in the frame she held over Top's face.

CHAPTER 15

Top was medical-evacuated that next morning.

Conscious and talking, he was sore as hell, and vomited a couple of times from the effects of the ether. But it couldn't be denied he was a hell of a lot better off after the slug was removed and the wound drained.

While waiting at the impromptu helicopter pad he'd even had a conversation with Ray Swift Elk who had taken over his top sergeant chores. The senior non-commissioned officer had left some very explicit instructions on how that particular office was to be operated in his absence.

Malpractice had carefully checked out his patient's blood pressure, pulse and temperature. The operation had steadied all the fluctuation in these vital signs, and the fever that had persisted since he was wounded, had actually gone away.

Top was still very weak, but the old fire was back in his eyes when Archie Dobbs and Calvin Culpepper loaded his litter aboard the H34 chopper that had flown up from Dak Bla to fetch him. The helicopter would carry the wounded sergeant major back to

Long Binh for the further, more complicated medical treatment that his war injury demanded.

After the chopper lifted off, Falconi watched it climb into the hot, blue sky. Then he turned to the detachment. "Move out!"

This sudden order surprised the watching villagers who had come out to observe the arrival and departure of the chopper. They watched as, per previous orders, the Black Eagles trotted back to their billets and reappeared with their full combat gear. Falconi's men hurried down to the river where their small flotilla waited.

Only Malpractice McCorckel tarried a bit.

He stopped by the hospital hut to say goodby to Jean. "I'll be back by day after tomorrow at the latest," he promised.

Her eyes were filled with tears. "Please, Malcomb. Be careful!"

The rugged Black Eagle looked down at the small woman. Her beauty and the compassion in the expression she showed him, touched him deeply. He set his gear down and gently put his hands on her face. Then he kissed her mouth.

Jean threw her arms around his neck and held on so tightly that he was forced to tenderly, but persistently pull himself free. Her voice quavered as she spoke. "Please—take care, Malcomb. I love you."

Malpractice hesitated, then he said, "I love you, Jean." He gave her another eye-to-eye gaze, then quickly picked up his equipment and turned to sprint for the boats.

There was another party interested in the departure. Choy, the Chinese-Vietnamese agent heard the commotion and the boats' engines being fired up. He stumbled sleepily out of the hut where he'd been resting up since his latest trek into the enemy hinter-

161

lands. When he saw the hurried activity, he came completely awake. "What happening? What happening?" he yelled out as he ran down to the river.

Archie Dobbs grinned at him from the command boat. "The war is starting up again, Choy. Wish us luck."

Choy's face was impassive. If he felt slighted because he had not been told of the coming action, he didn't show it. "Sure. Good luck, Black Eagles."

The small boat squadron eased out into the middle of the river, then turned north.

The captured NVA launch was manned by Chris Hawkins and his Alphas. The Bravo Team, under the command of Ray Swift Elk since Top's wound, were aboard their original boat with the steering gear now properly repaired.

Falconi, at his usual spot in the command boat with Archie and Chief Brewster, spoke into the AN/PRC-41's microphone. "Naughty Norski. This is Falcon. Over."

Erick Stensland's voice crackled over the speaker. "This is Naughty Norski. Over."

"Let's go. Over."

"We're on our way, Falcon. Out."

As Archie Dobbs would have stated so elegantly— The shit was about to hit the fan again.

Captain Ngy stood by the control console of his own command boat. He could see the lead boat in the NVA flotilla ahead. A glance backward showed that the other heavily armed craft was following closely.

The captain walked over to the DShK heavy machine gun. The gunner respectfully stepped aside as Ngy took the firing handles. He sighted straight ahead, then to each side as he swung the muzzle through its arc of fire. Lastly, he simulated aiming at an air attack. "*Tot*—good! The comrade mechanic did an excellent job in mounting the weapons."

The gunner smiled. "Yes, Comrade Captain. We will have a nasty surprise for the American helicopter if he is unwise enough to attack."

Ngy laughed. "Oh, indeed, he will be stupid enough to do so. In fact," he added, "I am counting on that." He returned to his post with a wide grin. Turning, he waved to the boat behind him. The troops aboard it gestured back with happy applause as was their custom.

Ngy was almost delirious in his joy.

Today there would be a great communist victory to enter in the glorious annals of world socialism.

Blue Richards' hands played lightly on the wheel as he maneuvered the Bravo boat through some floating tree limbs in the river. Swift Elk beside him was doubly vigilant.

They were the lead craft, traveling a bit more than fifty meters ahead of the Alpha boat and command boat. Their job was pure reconnaissance. Although expected to make first contact with the enemy, their orders were to withdraw quickly and inform the others of the situation. Too lightly armed to be of any real threat, they would act as scout and backup to the better equipped NVA boat that Archie and Blue had stolen several nights previously.

"You figger we'll git all the way up to the NVA camp?" Blue asked.

"We might," Swift Elk replied peering through his binoculars. "But we'll still run into a boat or two of theirs first."

Blue moved a bit more into mid-river. "You don't

163

like this kinda fightin', do you, Ray?"

Swift Elk shook his head. "It's too damned noisy. That's why the armored branch never appealed to me. It's fast and mean, but, man, things are continually roaring and belching."

"It's that Injun blood," Blue said.

"Prob'ly is," Swift Elk agreed, "my ancestors always make a helluva lot o' noise during the fighting, but they had some class when it came to getting to the battle site."

Calvin Culpepper, who had been listening, laughed. "The worst noise they had to worry about was their horses fartin', huh, Ray?"

Swift Elk grinned. "Or themselves maybe, Buffalo Soljer."

Malpractice, on the other side of the boat from Calvin hadn't heard a thing. His mind—indeed, his whole soul—was wrapped up in thoughts of Jean. The petite beauty had somehow penetrated the aura of toughness he'd thrown up around him. He'd kept worries, concerns for his buddies, sorrow over deaths, and other troublesome thoughts buried for a long time. These unpleasant thoughts were beginning to burst through now and then, but Jean was helping him get a handle on things once again.

"Enemy sighted!" Swift Elk yelled out.

Heavy machine gun fire splattered around as Blue made a hard turn to port. He pushed the throttle forward all the way, making the boat send up a wide spray of water.

Swift Elk spoke loudly into the Prick-Six radio. "Falconi. This is Bravo. We've made contact. Out!"

The moment he sighted the enemy boat, Ngy jumped on his radio. It was a short-range Soviet pack model, but it served his purposes well. He informed his other boats to form up for an attack.

In the meantime, his gunner went into action. He sighted in on the fleeing craft, pulling on the trigger of the heavy weapon in a rhythmic fashion. Well-aimed bursts of tracer rounds streaked toward the Black Eagle launch that now traveled so fast it seemed to want to lift itself from the friction of traveling over the river.

Whey Ngy's squadron was in the proper formation, he literally screamed his orders into the microphone:

"Tien len! Attack! Attack!"

Paulo Garcia put the NVA launch on top speed as he wheeled through the water to pass around the command boat.

Chris Hawkins held the twin firing mechanism that operated both starboard and port rocket tubes. Hank Valverde manned the Russian heavy machine gun. As a Special Forces qualified trooper, he was as much at home with this foreign weapon as he would have been with the American Browning fifty-caliber.

They waved to the Bravo boat as it sped past them to join up with Falconi, Archie and the chief. Within moments they sighted the NVA group. Hank swept the muzzle of the DShK back and forth as he laid out a curtain of fire.

"Line up on the bow of the lead craft," Chris said to Paulo.

"Aye, aye, sir!" the Marine acknowledged. "Dead on, sir."

Chris, with one eye closed, peered through the crude sight mounted on the control console. He aligned it with a similar one on the foredeck. When he was satisfied, he pushed the firing switch.

Both tubes roared as red fire flashed out the rear. The 40-millimeter rockets zipped forward and converged on the lead enemy craft. A roaring explosion erupted and the NVA boat's foredeck disintegrated. Within moments, after rapidly filling with water, it sank in the river, leaving the mangled remnants of its crew to float in the muddy water.

The Alpha boat zoomed in between the two surviving enemy launches. Paulo made a rapid turn while Chris laboriously reloaded the rocket tubes.

By then they'd gone beyond a bend in the river and were out of sight of their quarry. Paulo spared no speed to bring them back into the fight. But when they came around once more, the Alphas saw a sight they weren't expecting.

The enemy craft had also come about, and were rapidly charging back into them with heavy machine guns firing and rocket tubes loaded and ready.

Specialist Fourth Grade Olson sat in the front cockpit of the Cobra. Although he couldn't speak over the radio, he was tuned in so he could hear Chief Warrant Officer Stensland's exchanges with Falconi. When Gunnar wanted to talk to Stensland, he did so over the intercom.

Their earphones sparked loudly to life with Falconi's voice. "Naughty Norski. This is Falcon."

Stensland eagerly answered. "Roger, Falcon. Go ahead. Over."

"I have a mission for you. Over."

"The Naughty Norski is primed and waiting. Over," Stensland replied.

"Come on up the river," Falconi said. "There're NVA boats putting the pressure on just like we wanted. We got one but there's still two to go. Blow

166

'em away. Over."

"Wilco. Out," Stensland said. He spoke into the intercom. "Whattaya say, Gunnar?"

Gunnar the Gunner's voice was calm. "I'm ready."

"Hang on," Stensland said. The Naughty Norski flew up the river. When she passed over the command and Bravo boats, Stensland tipped to a nose down attitude for the attack.

The crew of the Alpha boat instinctively ducked.

Their foredeck exploded under incoming machine gun rounds, then a roaring explosion buffeted them on the starboard side. Chris watched the rocket tube mounted there fly off across the river to land in the jungle. At the same time the boat rolled violently to port, then went back the other way.

It didn't right itself.

"Aw, fuck!" Paulo yelled in frustration and anger. "We're sinking."

Chris jumped on the Prick-Six radio. "Falcon. This is Alpha. We've had it. Over."

Falconi's voice was calm. "Roger. Hang on. Naughty Norski is coming in. Out."

The two NVA boats had passed them, but quickly turned and started back. Chris was about to give orders to abandon ship when Stensland's helicopter gunship roared into view.

When the chopper was above them, its mini-gun suddenly began belching flaming hell at the NVA launches to the rear.

The water was now up to the Alpha's knees as they watched the Naughty Norski continue the attack. Then the chopper shuddered and pulled up in a shakey climb.

"*Dios salvanos!*" Hank Valverde exclaimed. "The

167

chopper's been hit!"

Falconi motioned to Chief Brewster to slow down as they approached the sinking Alpha boat. As they drew alongside, Hank and Ray Swift Elk leaped aboard. Chris Hawkins seemed to hesitate. He looked at the destroyed launch where he was now up to his waist in water. The expression on his face was pure anguish. "This is the second one I've lost!"

"Fuck it!" Falconi yelled. "Get aboard. We gotta get outta here."

"They damaged the chopper, sir," Chris reported breathlessly as he hopped onto the command boat.

"Are you sure?" Falconi asked.

Before anyone could answer, Chief Brewster leaped into action. "Here they come again!" He hit throttle and wheel as the two NVA boats came roaring at them from around the bend in the river.

"Naughty Norski. This is Falcon. Over."

No answer.

"Naughty Norski. This is Falcon. Do you read me? Over."

Still no reply.

"Try again, Skipper," Archie urged him. He pointed over the stern. "Those fuckers are really coming on fast."

"They're catching up with us!" Hank yelled.

Falconi again pressed the transmit button. "Naughty Norski! Naughty Norski! This is Falcon! This is Falcon! Over!"

The only sound that came over the radio was the hissing of dead air.

"The damned radio's hit," Stensland said in the

intercom.

Air buffeted Gunnar the Gunner's face from the shattered plexiglass windshield that had been blown apart by incoming rounds. "How's the engine sound?" he asked.

"Steady," Stensland said. "Want to make another run."

"*Ja* sure!" Gunnar said.

"Then let's give it a good Minnesota try," Stensland said. He cranked the throttle and pushed forward on the stick. Although she didn't respond to her controls with the old zip, the Naughty Norski dipped and headed back toward the surface of the river. When they zoomed over the Black Eagles, the crew caught a quick glimpse of Archie Dobbs waving at them from the foredeck of the command boat.

"I'll bet they're surprised to see us," Stensland remarked. "When they couldn't raise us on the radio, they probably figured we'd been blown out of the sky."

Gunnar didn't bother to make any statements. He remained silent as he sighted in the minigun once again. Finally he said, "Lower the nose."

Stensland complied and the gunship streaked in toward the NVA launches. The aircraft bucked a bit as the rapid-fire weapon spewed out a hailstorm of 7.62 millimeter slugs. Gunnar could see the enemy craft buck and shudder under the onslaught.

Then the rest of the windshield disintegrated and bits peppered off his facemask and helmet. "Pull up! Pull up!"

Stensland tried, but the chopper wouldn't respond. Instead, the Naughty Norski lazily went off to the right, losing altitude.

Gunnar turned and looked back. "What the hell's the matter?"

"We've had it," Stensland said grimly. "Brace yourself! We're going in."

Gunnar straightened up and looked down to see the tops of the trees rushing up at him.

"Uff da!"

CHAPTER 16

Ngy nervously smoked a cigarette as he sipped the hot green tea served him by his adjutant.

The afternoon's action had been a combination of exhilaration, terror and fear. The uplifting part had been when they'd sunk the boat captured from their patrol, but that victory had been overshadowed by the devastating attack from the helicopter. Ngy's other boat had been blown away, and even though they'd scored hits on the helicopter and seen it head down into the jungle, he had been unable to press on and destroy even the weakly-armed American launches.

Ngy's own command boat had been so badly damaged that he'd been unable to continue the fight. He'd been forced to ignominiously return to his base at half-speed astern while his gunner kept the DShK's muzzle ready for any attack—no matter how improbable.

The adjutant had also poured himself a cup of the hot brew. He sat down at the table with his commander. "What further actions will be taken, Comrade Captain?"

Ngy lit another cigarette off the burning stub of the first. He sucked in the smoke and exhaled. "Even at this moment I am planning our next mission, Comrade Adjutant." He noted his hands were still shaking.

The other officer's face was set and grim. "Our comrade soldiers desire vengeance," he said. "They are eager to return to combat."

"I am aware of that," Ngy said. Under normal circumstances, the NVA captain's own morale would have been all but destroyed. He had one consolation, however, and he glanced out the window of his headquarters to the river at a sight that made him feel a hell of a lot better. "We still have three more heavily armed river boats waiting to be used against the Black Eagles."

The adjutant smiled and poured them both another cupful. "The agent Tho May will be here soon. He will have a complete and accurate report on the actual fighting capabilities of those American gangsters."

"You are right, of course, Comrade Adjutant." Ngy took a drink of the tea as his mood began to mellow out. The duel on the Song Cai was far from over, and he was better equipped to gain a victory than was the American commander.

The two deuce-and-a-half trucks pulled up to the military docks at Dak Bla. Chuck Fagin got out of the passenger side of the lead vehicle and smiled a greeting to the ARVN major who had come out to meet them.

"*Chao ong*, my friend," Fagin said.

The major was a bit surprised by the stocky American dressed in a manner that was not quite military regulation. "*Chao ong*, what is it that I may do to serve you?"

"Well, now, I have a transportation problem," Fagin said a bit taken back by the man's complicated English. "And I think you can help me."

"If such a thing is possible, then I shall perform the favor with great pleasure," the major said, displaying a toothy grin.

"Do you recall the American unit that recently passed through here and went north up the Song Cai there?" Fagin asked pointing at the river.

"Are you speaking, perhaps, of the gentlemens who have gained ownership of several river patrol boats?" the major asked.

"The same," Fagin answered. "I believe they went to the village of Tam Nuroc."

"Ah, yes!" the major said. "You are most absolutely correct."

"Well, I have a delivery for them," he said pointing at the trucks. "If you'll lend me the use of one of your river boats, I'll take the stuff they need up to them."

The major's face assumed an expression of genuine regret. "Alas! Alas! For that is not possible that favor to perform. My river boats are undertaking orders to patrol to the south. Not one cannot be spared, and I have only three."

Fagin didn't quite understand what the man meant. "You're saying you can't?"

"It is that exactly that I am saying at you," the major said. "I am sorry. Yes. Very and truly and really sorry."

"Yeah. I appreciate your feelings, really, Major. But the guys have to have this shipment. Without it, their mission will fail."

The major's face brightened. "It is an idea I have

for you if you will but permit me to say it out loud."

"Certainly," Fagin said. "Say it out loud by all means."

"The Americans that go north have boats," the major said. "I have a radio. You can talk at them and say to come and get what it is you have to bestow upon them."

Fagin shook his head. "Nope. I can't do that. It's too big a security risk to broadcast to them from here. Even in code, it would catch the attention of any NVA or VC monitoring the transmissions."

The major wrung his hands and became so sorrowful that Fagin thought he was going to cry. "But, oh, horrors! I have my orders. Not one boat can be given up for this and I have but three."

"Please," Fagin said. "It's absolutely necessary. And I'm afraid I'll need your other two boats to come along as escorts."

"All three? Such a thing is so absurd as to be not able to accomplish," the ARVN major insisted.

"You gotta do it," Fagin said. "There's no question about refusing."

"Oh, forgive me, dear friend!" the major wailed. "I regret the action I cannot take."

Fagin took the major by the arm and led him off to one side where neither the truck drivers nor the ARVN troops nearby could hear. The CIA man spoke softly but directly to the point. "I'll give you a refrigerator."

The major's eyes widened. "American refrigerator?"

"There is a luxury model General Electric in the back of that second truck, Major. It's yours for a trip up to Tam Nuroc."

The major smiled. "You need men for to help you

put your goods upon the boat of my unit?"

Fagin grinned back. "Does Raggedy Andy have cotton balls?"

"What is the meaning of what you have spoken at me?"

"That means I need men to put the stuff on your launch."

"Right away you want this done?"

Fagin nodded. "Let's not waste time, okay?"

Tam Nuroc's militia chief — and the people he served — were again agitated and upset over the Black Eagles' return from combat.

Another boat had been obviously lost, and the others were badly shot up once again. The citizen solider Trang wasted no time in going to Lieutenant Colonel Falconi's headquarters for another briefing on the situation. Falconi didn't bother to paint the proverbial pretty picture.

"We got mauled again," he told Trang. "The one boat that had the heavy weaponry we needed was sunk by the enemy. I'd hoped that we could get a couple more of their launches, but it didn't work out."

Trang nervously wiped his mouth with his hands. "But you still have the *may bay turc-thang*, true?"

"It was shot down," Falconi said.

"Destroyed?"

"I'm afraid so."

Trang was thoughtful for several moments. "What if the enemy attacks us?"

"We'll be in a bad way, I'm afraid," Falconi said. "But don't worry. My men and I will not leave you alone."

Trang forgot his correct Oriental deportment for a moment. "Your presence will make not one bit of difference. The village will be destroyed."

"We will stand beside you," Falconi assured him.

"Will you die with us?" Trang asked.

"If necessary."

Again Trang was silent for several moments. Then he stood up. *"Chao ong."*

"Chao ong," Falconi said.

The militia captain took his leave.

Swift Elk walked over. "That was pretty brief."

Falconi shrugged. "There wasn't a hell of lot that either of us could say."

Swift Elk wasn't satisfied. "Trang took things a bit too calmly to suit me."

"He wouldn't want to lose face by expressing any fear he felt," Falconi said.

"Either that," Swift Elk surmised, "or he's damned pleased with the way things are going."

Tho May showed up at the NVA camp quite late that night. From his appearance it was obvious he'd done some rapid and ceaseless travel through the jungle. Even with help from local VC units, the journey had taken its toll. His face was drawn and haggard, and he accepted cold water and a bowl of fish and rice from Captain Ngy before he began to talk.

"The Americans are close to being beaten," he said.

Ngy was enthusiastic. "Is their morale destroyed? Too many casualties?"

Tho May shook his head. "No. They are not the sort of fighters who would fold under pressure. Yet they are ill-equipped. You must move south and wipe them out as quickly as possible."

"My men are standing by," Ngy said. "But it is too dark to travel safely on the river. There is much floating debris."

Tho May finished the soup and pushed the bowl away. "Hit them as early as possible, Comrade. Neither they nor the village militia is capable of withstanding a well-armed assault."

Ngy nodded. "Besides the boats, I have numerous infantrymen to storm the village."

Tho May stood up. "My presence is required elsewhere. In the meantime, I will keep you informed as much as I can." He stood up and looked straight into Ngy's eyes. "You realize, of course, Comrade Captain, that I will be making a full report on your conduct to higher headquarters."

Ngy snarled. "I do not fight from fear of criticism by my superiors, Comrade. I carry on the struggle because of my unrelenting devotion to Marxism and world socialism."

"Most admirable," Tho May said. "But there is no reason for unpleasant emotions, Comrade. You will be going to an easy victory. But don't worry. There will still be a decoration in it for you."

"I like dead Americans better than medals," Ngy said.

Tho May laughed to lighten the moment. "Then you should be a very happy man before mid-morning tomorrow." He walked to the door. "*Chao ong*, comrade. *Chuc ong may man*—good luck!"

Ngy watched the man disappear into the surrounding jungle, then he yelled for his adjutant. "Fall out the men fully armed and have them stand by for the rest of the night aboard the boats. We strike at first light!"

Malpractice lay on the sleeping pallet with his arm around Jean. He'd just finished a four-hour stint on guard duty and his eyes ached with the weariness of watchful waiting.

Jean shifted her position so she could put her head on his chest. "They say your helicopter is shot down."

"Yeah," Malpractice said. His voice was soft and somber. "And two good guys are lost out in the jungle."

"Will you go to find them, Malcomb?"

"Naw," he replied. "The colonel don't figger it'd do any good and he's right. The place is crawling with Charlies. Any search parties would be policed up and made pris'ners too."

"It is sad," Jean said.

"It sure as hell is," Malpractice said. "I doubt if they're alive though. The crew is prob'ly burned to cinders in the wreckage of their aircraft."

"You get too upset, Malcomb," Jean said.

"Maybe so. You'd think I'd get used to it. But ever'time one o' the guys gets hurt or killed, it takes a little more out of me."

Jean caressed his face with her little hand. "You are a—a—well, in French the word would be *sympathique*."

Malpractice only nodded and continued to stare up at the ceiling of the hut.

"I know you are a very worried man," Jean said. "It is easy to see."

"How?" Malpractice asked.

Jean's voice was hesitant. "It is that you have not made love to me."

"Shit!" Malpractice sat up.

"I am sorry, Malcomb. I did not mean to make you angry."

The Black Eagle medic got to his feet and walked to the door. He stood there looking out into the dark village. "That's all I goddamned well needed. To be reminded o' that."

Jean joined him, putting an arm around his waist. "It is nothing to worry about, Malcomb. It is nice. Because you come to see me anyway."

He smiled down at her. "I'm sorry."

"I love you, Malcomb."

"I love you too, Jean."

They stood in silence for several long minutes before their reverie was interrupted by soft footsteps approaching the hut. Malpractice tensed, then recognized the shadow coming toward them. "Hi, Archie."

"Hi ya, Malpractice," Archie Dobbs said. "Hi, Jean. How're you doing?"

Jean pressed protectively closer to her lover. "I am fine, thank you."

"Malpractice," Archie said. "The Falcon wants to see you." He turned and walked away, pausing only to add, "he says immediately if not sooner."

"Okay. I'm on my way."

Malpractice kissed Jean, then went to get his M16 before leaving the hut and hurrying down to the headquarters shack.

Falconi and Swift Elk were leaning over a quickly drawn sketch map of the village. The lieutenant colonel looked up when Malpractice came into the room. "How're the medical supplies, Malpractice?"

"We ain't used much. Only on Top. Why?"

"The NVA boat unit is going to hit us as sure as shit stinks," Falconi said. "We won't be able to do much but hold on and hope for relief."

179

"How does the chance for help look?" Malpractice asked.

"Not good," Swift Elk interjected. "The closest outfit is that ARVN unit at Dak Bla. We're cornered here, so even with gunship support we're facing some bad odds."

"How about a withdrawal through the jungle?"

"We could do that," Falconi said. "But the villagers would be slaughtered after we left."

"Couldn't they go with us?" Malpractice asked.

Falconi shook his head. "There's too many of 'em. And since the VC own that territory between here and Dak Bla, we wouldn't stand any chance at all with a crowd like that. Hell, there's more women and kids than men. So we'll stick here and punch it out with the help of the local militia. There'll be a lot of casualties."

"I'm getting tired o' this shit," Malpractice said calmly.

"Ease up," Swift Elk warned him.

But Malpractice didn't seem too excited despite the anger in his words. "It's that old song and dance we're always hearing," he said in perfect control. "The brass have been wanting to wipe us out for a long time."

"You don't believe that, do you?" Swift Elk asked.

"After all we've been through?" Malpractice said with a mirthless grin. "You goddamned right I believe it!"

"Jesus Christ, Malpractice!" Falconi snapped. "There's always hope!"

"No way, sir," Malpractice said. "This time we're going out on the floor for the last waltz." He thought of Jean. "At least I got a pretty partner." He laughed at Falconi. "All you got is the Injun." He left them and walked back out into the night.

180

Falconi and Swift Elk looked at each other. The lieutenant colonel forced a grin. "He's right about one thing. You're not as good looking as Jean."

Swift Elk smiled back at his commander. "And he's not wrong on another."

"What's that?" Falconi asked.

"Our shit is weak."

CHAPTER 17

Malpractice McCorckel sat against the *rurng* tree watching the jungle's darkness fade away under the slow onslaught of the coming day's light.

Although he'd been on the post for four hours, he was just as alert as he had been when he'd first relieved Paulo Garcia after the Marine's stint as sentinel. Malpractice's M16 was cradled in his arms while he let his eyes and ears drink in the change in the environment around him.

The night creatures' sounds—their calls and rustlings—faded away while the awakening prowlers of the day took over the primitive environment where the slow and the weak died fast to feed their betters.

Malpractice was turned into it all, as wrapped up in nature as Ray Swift Elk's ancestors ever were.

There were vibrations perceived by his senses that brought him into the natural surroundings, and the medic felt as if he were not only the master of his own fate, but of this domain which he ruled with his superior intellect and 5.56 millimeter rifle.

When the light was bright enough, Malpractice lit a cigarette and slowly exhaled. The taste and smell of the tobacco was wonderful after so many hours without smoking. He smoked languidly and thoughtfully as his being sank deeper into the jungle's pulse.

Suddenly he tensed—those same senses now screaming to his psyche of danger. Someone was moving toward him.

"Calcitra—"

Malpractice recognized Blue Richard's accent in the challenge. He immediately replied with the password.

"Clunis."

Blue approached silently until he found him. His voice was a coarse whisper. "Hi ya, Malpractice. You can scat now."

"Whew," Malpractice replied. "I was getting stiff." He stood up and climbed out of the shallow fighting hole. "Today is gonna be a hot one."

"No shit," Blue agreed. "But ain't they all?" He wasted no time in taking over the guard post.

"There ain't much to report," Malpractice said. He pointed to the north. "The village militia still has a sentry over there. I could hear him snoring."

Blue laughed. "A lack o' dedication."

Malpractice failed to see any humor in the situation. "You'd think the sonofabitch would worry about the VC moving in. I wonder how he'd like to see his old lady raped 'til her eyes popped out."

"I don't figger he'd like that," Blue said settling himself into a more comfortable position. "But that points out the main differ'nce between us and them, ol' buddy. And that keyword is discipline—di-sci-pline!"

183

The medic wasn't interested in discussing the merits of regular troops over civilian militia. "I guess I'll get on back to my hootch," Malpractice said.

"Okay, Malpractice. See you later." Then Blue spoke again. "Can I ask you somethin'?"

"Sure."

Blue grinned. "Are you sweet on that village gal who helped you out with Top?"

Malpractice spoke the words that conveyed a clear message from one male to another: "She's a nice girl."

"She sure seems to be," Blue responded correctly.

"So long, Blue."

Malpractice walked slowly down the path that led back to Tam Nuroc. He went directly to the headquarters tent to report in. Rapping on the door, he stuck his head inside. "I'm properly relieved."

Ray Swift Elk looked up from cleaning his weapon. "Come in, Malpractice. I want to talk to you."

Malpractice accepted the invitation and stepped in. "Where's Falconi?"

"Down at the river," Swift Elk said.

Malpractice went over to the commanding officer's chair and sat down. "Four hours in a hole is a long time."

"Sure is," Swift Elk said still working on his rifle. "You feeling okay?"

"I'm fine," Malpractice said. "How come you're asking? Do I look sick or something?"

"No. I'm just acting like a team leader," Swift Elk said. "I haven't been in this job too long to have you guys checked out."

"Don't worry about me," Malpractice said. "How're the other guys? Blue seems all right."

184

"We're a hunnerd percent," Swift Elk said.

Malpractice peered at him. "Is there something you want to ask me about?"

"Yeah—" Swift Elk hesitated. He ran a cleaning rod down the barrel of the M16. "Forget it. It wasn't nothing important."

Malpractice stood up. "Then I'll be getting back to my hootch."

"Sure. See you later."

"Yeah. Later," Malpractice said. He left the hut and went back down the street to the village dispensary. Jean still had it closed up tight to conserve the night coolness for as long as possible. He quickly slipped through the door and shut it.

Jean lay on their double sleeping mat. She had awakened at his entrance. She slowly brushed back her long, raven-black hair with her small hands and looked up at him. "Good morning, Malcomb."

"Hi, Jean. Sleep well?"

"Yes, thank you." She moved over to make room for him. "Now you get some sleep."

He noticed she was naked under the thin linen sheet that covered her as he stripped off his web gear and peeled away his jungle fatigues.

Jean laughed. "You look funny without clothes except for your boots."

Malpractice grinned. "I guess I do." He divested himself of the footgear, then joined her on the mat. He yawned and glanced over at the young woman beside him. The sheet had fallen away, exposing her firm breasts. Malpractice reached over and cupped one in his hand, his long, sensitive fingers gently kneading a nipple.

Jean breathed harder and rolled over to kiss him.

185

When Malpractice took his hand away, she grasped it and laid it back where it was. She noticed a movement under the sheet, and reached down to note that Malpractice was responding to her beauty. Jean slowly pulled the flimsy cover off them both, and manipulated his manhood.

"Oh, Malcomb! You want me." She lay back and pulled him over on top of her.

"Yeah," Malpractice said. "I want you."

He made love to her for the first time. He did it slow and gently as she grasped at him with both arms and legs. Jean kissed him wildly, thrusting her tongue into his mouth.

Then he stiffened and she pushed back at him until they both shuddered to a climax. They stayed coupled for another few moments until Jean reluctantly allowed him to withdraw and lay back on his side of the mat.

"That wasn't much," Malpractice said.

"It was wonderful, Malcomb."

"I'll do better next time," he said. "It'll last longer. I ain't been with a woman in quite a while. When we —"

"Malcomb," she interrupted.

"Yes?" he answered.

"I am your woman."

"Jean."

"Yes?"

Malpractice smiled. "That's the best thing that's happened to me." Then he added, "In my whole life."

"Me too, Malcomb."

They smiled at each other and settled back under the sheet.

The young boy squatted on his haunches and absent-mindedly watched the float on the end of his fishing line bob on the surface on the Song Cai.

His name was Duy, and like most river children, his childhood had been unmercifully short. As soon as he was able he began to contribute to the support of the family. At first this was done by helping the women in their various chores. He ran errands for his mother, helped in threshing the rice stalks after harvest, did a bit of carrying and hauling, and other light tasks. When he was large enough—and strong enough—he graduated to working with his father and the other men in the rice paddies.

Duy had finally worked his way up to tending the water buffalo that pulled the crude wooden plows when an unexpected opportunity presented itself for another kind of work. This was not only easier physically, but it paid cash. With one of their group having a job like that, the family could go to Tam Nuroc on market day and do more than barter and trade; they could actually buy items they wanted.

The new employment was as a servant in the pleasure house of Madame Fleurette Hue. He did odd jobs that were continually popping up on the premises. Most were too heavy for a woman yet too light for a man—but just right for a twelve-year-old boy like Duy.

Even the fishing he was enjoying at the moment was being performed as a chore assigned him by Madame Fleurette. Fish was an important staple in the diet of the pleasure girls. Madame Fleurette knew that it kept them from getting too fat and unattractive, so she sent Duy out to the river almost daily. Of course there was an additional task to the diversion. Duy was to keep an eye on the river, and if he saw anything unusual or strange, particularly where soldiers were involved, he was to run back to the house and immediately inform his mistress.

Duy's mind was on other things too. He knew exactly what the pleasure house was for, and he marvelled at the fact that men would actually give money to girls to mate with them. But there were rather nice sides to the work too. Several of Madame Fleurette's prostitutes had told him he was a pretty boy who would grow up to be a handsome man. When he became an adult, he could have girls working for him. They would like him very much, the women said, and would give him all their money. Duy was practical enough to recognize that not only was that better than being a peasant or river fisherman, it paid a hell of a lot more too. He had decided it would be worth it even if he didn't particularly like girls.

His thoughts were interrupted by the sound of several boats drawing near. Duy looked up from his fishing expecting to see the soldiers pull into the little dock on the river and spend some more money on those silly women. But instead of stopping, they continued on past the whorehouse. Duy also noted they seemed different from their usual appearance. They carried more guns and there were many more of them than usual aboard their launches.

Surely this was unusual enough to inform Madame Fleurette.

Duy left his line and ran back to the house. He found his employer in her office. *"Chao ba,"* he greeted her respectfully.

Fleurette had just been through an ordeal with one

of the girls who was a chronic complainer. She was not in a good mood. But the woman liked Duy, and controlled her irritation. "What is it, *trai*?"

"The soldiers from the north go down the river," Duy said.

Fleurette had a headache. She gently rubbed her temples with both hands. "Yes. They do that often."

"But they have lots of guns," Duy said frowning.

"That is true," Fleurette said. "They always do."

"But, Madame Fleurette! They have many, many guns!"

She was suddenly interested. "More than usual?"

Duy vigorously nodded his head. "Yes! Yes! And there are more of them on their boats."

Fleurette reached out and grabbed the boy by both shoulders. "Listen to me, Duy. I am going to write a note. I want you to take it through the jungle to Tam Nuroc as fast as you can go."

Duy frowned. "That is a long way!"

"I know. But this is important," Madame Fleurette said. "You find the Americans that are there and give them the note."

"I cannot speak with them," Duy said. "I don't know their language."

"It has been told to me that their chief speaks our tongue perfectly," Madame Fleurette said impatiently. "He will have no trouble understanding you. Besides, all you have to do is hand over the note."

"I will have to run and run and run and run to beat the boats there," Duy complained.

Fleurette struck his face. "Then *chay*, little one, run! Run!"

Duy immediately realized this was of great importance to her. He regretted his reluctance to obey her.

The madame got her paper and pen. She wrote rapidly in French explaining that from all appearances, the NVA were going to attack Tam Nuroc. When she finished, she folded it tightly and placed it in one of the pockets of his short pants. "Do not tarry!"

"I will obey you, Madame!" Duy rushed out the door and turned down the path, his short legs pumping as he settled into a rapid trot that would do credit to a full-grown infantryman.

The path he took was well worn. It traveled along a route between the scattered villages and led south several kilometers to a spot where there was a bridge over the Song Cai. Once across it, the rest of the journey was easier and quicker into Tam Nuroc.

But Duy's journey was interrupted.

A man stepped out from the jungle onto the path and grabbed him. "Wait up, boy!"

Duy fearfully looked into the face of a man he'd seen at the pleasure house several times. His uneasiness melted away. "Oh! *chao ong*, Tho May."

Tho May, the Red agent, didn't relax his tight grip on the boy's shoulders. "What is your name, boy?"

"Duy," he answered. "You know me. I work for Madame Fleurette."

"To be sure," Tho May said. "And why are you running so rapidly down this path?"

"I am on an errand for Madame Fleurette," Duy answered.

"What sort of errand, boy?"

"I go to Tam Nuroc to deliver a message to the Americans there," Duy said.

"I see," Tho May said. "Well, I am going to Tam Nuroc. You tell me the message and I shall deliver it

190

for you."

But Duy shook his head. "I don't think I should."

Tho May snarled. "Tell me the message, boy!"

Duy was frightened again. "She only wanted to let them know that the soldiers from the north were going to visit them."

"I will tell them."

"I must obey my mistress," Duy insisted.

"If I do her bidding, she will be just as well served," Tho May argued. "Now go back to Madame Fleurette."

"With respect, Tho May," Duy said uneasily. "But I cannot."

"I said return to your mistress, boy," Tho May said angrily.

"No!"

Duy jerked himself free and made an attempt to run around the man. But Tho May was quick. He regained his grasp on the boy's clothing and flung him hard against a nearby tree.

"You little bastard!"

Duy bounced back and fell on the path. There was a deep gash on his forehead. His mind swirled within his tiny head as he tried to grasp the terrible, surprising thing that had just happened.

He never had time to ponder it much.

The knife went into the small body and did massive damage with each twist. It didn't take long to drain away Duy's life blood.

Tho May wiped the weapon clean, then picked up the dead child and flung the body into the forest where the animals would feast on the corpse before it rotted away.

Then the agent rushed through the trees to the river

to see if he could catch sight of the NVA boats. When he got there he was able to spot the stern of the last boat in the convoy as it disappeared around a bend in the waterway.

Tho May smiled to himself.

The village of Tam Nuroc would be catching hell within a very short time.

CHAPTER 18

The mid-morning guard relief was well settled in. Both the local militia and the Black Eagle sentries sat idly at their posts, feeling relaxed and a bit bored.

The night hours were the most exciting time for that sort of duty in the jungle. Combining the natural noises of falling vegetation, breezes and prowling animals with men's fertile imaginations made for hours filled with suspense during the darkest periods. That was also the time that small groups of VC like to pull lightning quick hits on individual positions leaving one or two men dead before melting back into the inky blackness that concealed them so well.

But mid-morning to early evening was a time to let up a bit. The visibility was great—except where the monsoon forest was the thickest—and the general activity around gave a sense of security and well-being to even the most alert guards.

The militia sentries were dozing, and a couple were actually into a deep sleep, their soft snoring blending in with the buzzing of the insects. Alpha Team, made up of Chris Hawkins, Calvin Culpepper and Hank Valverde, was on post. Though not sleeping in any sense of the word, they were mentally goofing off as the afternoon heat pressed in with greater and greater intensity.

Then the 12.7 millimeter rounds exploded into the trees.

Screams from a couple of militiamen showed they had borne the brunt of the incoming fire. The three Black Eagles instinctively ducked their heads as the concussion created by the enemy fusillade made their ears ache and ring.

Calvin and Hank immediately returned fire while Chris got hold of Falconi on the Prick-Six. "Falcon. This is Alpha. NVA troops are in the jungle in front of us. Can't tell how many. We're getting hit hot and heavy, but holding right now. Out." Then the Navy lieutenant joined in the battle.

The first NVA appeared through the trees and drew the Alphas' undivided attention which consisted of several well-placed fire bursts of 5.56 millimeter fire. A couple of the Reds pitched to the ground while their buddies pulled back. Then incoming rocket grenades blasted around the Black Eagles.

Calvin, as grenadier, did his best to match the enemy efforts with his own M203 launcher, but he was badly outnumbered. Finally the militia positions to the left collapsed and the NVA turned their full attention on the Americans.

Chris made a quick tactical decision. "Get the fuck out of here!" he yelled.

The pressure from the attacking forces was so great that the team was forced completely out of the jungle to the village. They linked up with the command element and Bravo Team who were also catching hell.

Trang, the militia captain, joined Falconi at the time the battle went into its second quarter hour. He wasted no time on empty courtesy or custom. "I cannot find where the enemy is attacking from, Colonel. I have sent a small patrol forward, but they did not return."

"I believe the NVA came ashore from river boats," Falconi said. "So they may have more aboard to hit us from another side of the village. I am worried about your people."

"Colonel Falconi, I have ordered the non-combatants evacuated into the jungle."

Falconi was pleased with the news. It gave him more room to work. "How long will it be before they're out of the combat area?"

"They have already gone," Trang announced. "Now my men and I shall fight like tigers to save them from the clutches of the NVA bastards."

"Good, Captain Trang," Falconi said. "We'll do the same. I hope you have established a defensive perimeter to the west of the village."

"That is exactly what I have done, Colonel."

"Thank you, Captain. Please hold tight there until further orders."

Trang saluted, then rushed off to obey the orders. Falconi gave the South Vietnamese a thumbs up, then called in his team leaders. Chris and Swift Elk left the line and reported in to him.

"Trang and the militia are to the west and dug in," Falconi told them. "We're going to hit the NVA and try to drive them out that way. The militia isn't real professional, but there's plenty of 'em and they're motivated to kick some ass."

Chris wasn't enthusiastic. "We need something heavy to back us up, sir."

"I agree," Swift Elk interjected.

195

"So do I," Falconi said. "But we don't have a single support weapon — mortar or machine gun — and there's not a goddamned thing I can do about it. With a bit of luck we might overrun a couple of their positions and grab some heavier weaponry."

"We'll pass the word for the guys to work on that."

"In the meantime," Falconi said. "Let's hit the sons of bitches."

It took less than five minutes for the attack to be mounted. The Black Eagles struck out and slugged their way forward a few meters. The heavy enemy fire slowed them, but they continued to press on, firing effectively. The 40-millimeter grenades that Calvin Culpepper and Paulo Garcia contributed to the effort added to the volley giving them at least a bit more punch.

Then the militia to the west broke away under intense attack from the NVA in that sector. They retreated back to a stronger position. This left the Black Eagles standing alone and isolated.

The NVA swept their rockets and heavy machine guns full bore onto the Americans. Falconi barely got the guys back into the village before their former position was turned into a miniature wasteland of blasted trees and slug-plowed earth.

There was less cover here, but the fields of fire were greatly improved. The lead NVA elements charged in out of the tree line and were blown away by well-coordinated volleys from the Black Eagles who were able to freely utilize their overlapping sweeps of volleys.

But the NVA's superior firepower came to the front, and the village seemed overwhelmed by rockets, heavy machine gun fire and light weapons fusillades that again put pressure on Falconi and his men.

"Withdraw through the huts to the other side and

turn back when we're in the tree line," Falconi yelled.

The Black Eagles performed the maneuver superbly, inflicting more casualities until they were into the relative safety of the jungle.

Ray Swift Elk, off on the right flank, hit the transmit button on his Prick-Six. "Falcon. This is Bravo. The NVA units in the village are disorganized and hesitating."

Falconi realized the enemy's initial success had a hell of an element of luck in it. He decided to kick their butts a little. "Alpha. Bravo. We'll hit the place again. Move out."

The attack startled the unsure NVA who were beginning to wander around trying to pull their formation back together. Broken up and uncoordinated, the Black Eagle assault was ferocious and demoralizing.

The NVA ran.

Captain Ngy stood at the control console of his boat. He hadn't had a situation report for a full ten minutes. He glanced right and left, noting that his reserve troops were ready and eager to join the fight.

"Company commanders!" he screamed into his microphone. "Report in! Report in!"

Within a few moments he knew that his attack, which had initially succeeded, had unraveled and was getting chewed up. He looked at the eager young commander of the second wave. Ngy bellowed at him:

"*Tien len!* Attack!"

Swift Elk's Bravos were enjoying a growing degree of success. Their fusillades had been so accurate that they were forced to leap over fallen NVA as they forced the enemy back into the jungle.

Archie Dobbs had left the command element to get into his favorite spot—the front. He was a few paces ahead of Swift Elk, advancing at a steady walk as he swept the thick foliage ahead of him with steady bursts of fire. He glanced to his right and slowed to allow Malpractice to draw alongside of him. Archie grinned viciously. "Looks like we'll pull this one out."

Malpractice, thinking of Jean out in the jungle with the other women and the children, had fought with spectacular ferocity. He wasn't interested in winning the battle for any patriotic or tactical reasons—he was a man protecting his woman from the enemy, and the sooner all the bastards were either dead or fleeing, the better he would feel.

Archie noticed his friend rushing on forward. "Hey, Malpractice! Slow down! You're gonna get so far ahead you'll be sniper bait."

Malpractice finished hosing out the last of a magazine. As he slammed another into its place he looked over at Archie. "Move out, goddamnit! We ain't gonna run them sonofabitches off acting like pussies."

"Pussies!" Archie yelled back. "*Pussies!* What the fuck you want, shithead? A goddamned suicide charge?"

"Whatever it takes," Malpractice said resuming his rapid advance forward.

Then the proverbial shit hit the proverbial fan.

The reinforcements from the boats on the river joined the battle. They swept ahead gathering up their disorganized and retreating comrades. NCOs kicked and pummeled these demoralized elements back into cohesive units, then ordered them forward.

Malpractice McCorckel, continuing his reckless

charge, was the first Black Eagle to make contact. An NVA group appeared to his front, and Malpractice gave them half a magazine of automatic fire. But he received an incoming small arms volley from his left—then his right. Infuriated, he stupidly ran out of ammo trying to fight to both sides.

Archie Dobbs joined him and provided covering fire for both while they pulled back to the main body. "Well, so much for your fucking *banzai* charge," he said between pulls on his M16 trigger. They had fallen far enough to the rear to be between the Alphas and Bravos by then.

"I'm running outta ammo," Malpractice snarled.

"I ain't surprised," Archie said pulled a bandoleer off his shoulder and handing it over to the medic. "You been shooting like bullets was going outta style."

Malpractice pulled a magazine from one of the cloth pockets and loaded it into the M16 without bothering to answer. As far as he was concerned, he was doing exactly as he should.

However, Archie was concerned. "You be careful, Malpractice. You're gonna get blowed away."

Malpractice pulled back on the charging handle and seated the first round. "Then I'll be joining some pretty select comp'ny."

Before Archie could reply, the entire force of the NVA's renewed attack rolled over both teams.

Falconi raised the Prick-Six to order a retreat, but the small radio exploded in his hands as an AK-47 round smashed into it. However, electronic communications weren't necessary in the confined space of the battle. Both the Alphas and Bravos were pushed in by the enveloping formation of the attack.

"Ray!" Falconi yelled at Swift Elk. "Lay down some heavy cover!"

The Sioux Indian's team responded quickly to his orders. Calvin Culpepper's M203 pumped out 40-millimeter grenades as fast as he could work the weapon. Malpractice, as automatic rifleman, swept their front and flanks with a steady measure of short bursts, while Blue and Archie—an uninvited but welcome guest—concentrated on single-shot fire that was slower but a lot more accurate.

Chris Hawkins formed up Paulo Garcia, Hank Valverde and Chief Brewster to move back steadily behind this curtain of steel hail. When they reached a relatively good defensive position they stopped.

Now Falconi needed a Prick-Six. He grabbed Chris' radio, and spoke calmly into the mouthpiece. "Bravo, this is Falcon. Move back through our lines."

It was basic fire and maneuver by the book.

A green or poorly-disciplined unit could hardly hope for success. But superbly trained, professional military men like Lieutenant Colonel Falconi commanded, could hold off superior numbers for a time before being overwhelmed.

The trick was timing.

Swift Elk's guys joined the others. This temporary grouping allowed a marked increased in defensive firing that would slow and demoralize the attackers for a bit. But the NVA combat leaders were experienced and soon had made a running reorganization—applied with a bit of ass-kicking—and their assault resumed in its former intensity.

The Bravos, by Falconi's orders, pulled out of the formation and moved backward again. Then the Alphas did likewise as the unit withdrew toward the cover offered by the village.

Again there was a link-up and a fresh increase of firepower that ripped apart the NVA's front ranks. Enemy bodies piled up for a brief minute before the

Black Eagles made a final retrograde maneuver that carried them into Tam Nuroc.

Falconi quickly established the unit in the defense posture he wanted. The Alphas held the right of the line, the Bravos the left. A brief firefight broke out as advanced elements of the NVA probed forward to check out the Americans.

Then the battle ebbed a bit, until it fell silent.

"Fresh magazines!" Falconi yelled. "Lock and load, guys. This is the lull before the storm."

"Colonel Falconi! Colonel Falconi!"

Falconi turned at the sound of his name and saw Trang, the leader of the militia, running through the huts toward him. He was glad to see the brave South Vietnamese. When the man arrived, Falconi quickly returned the formal salute rendered. "We need bolstering here, Captain Trang. Please bring your men forward."

Trang sadly shook his head. "I am sorry, *Trung-ta*. Most of my men are dead. We desperately need help."

Falconi's head snapped back to the front where a roaring explosion of incoming automatic fire announced the opening of the NVA attack. He looked back at Trang. "I'm outgunned and outnumbered myself, *Ban*."

Trang, despite the danger of the situation, smiled in pleasure at being referred to as friend. "There is an old Vietnamese saying that perhaps will comfort you."

"I need encouraging words," Falconi said.

"A trapped tiger is not a dead one," Trang said. "Perhaps that thought will give you some encouragement."

"We Black Eagles have a saying of our own that we use whether we're winning or losing," Falconi replied. "It's a basic philosophy, inelegant and crude, but it works for us."

"What is that, *Trung-Ta*?"

"*Calcitra clunis*—Kick ass."

The the NVA assault exploded out of the jungle and swept forward into the village.

CHAPTER 19

The initial NVA advance into the Black Eagles was by rifle squads. Formed into skirmish lines, they tested and probed, exchanged shots and took a few casualties that were left sprawled in the open space between the tree line and the outlying village huts.

Falconi's guys had plenty of bullets and rocket grenades—the only problem was the one that had plagued them since the beginning of the operation: the munitions were too goddamned light. With the heaviest thing they could throw at the enemy being the 40-millimeter loads out of Calvin and Paulo's M203s, they were woefully underarmed.

The NVA commander, now tired of expending casualties in the rolling combat that had see-sawed back and forth through the jungle, brought up his mortars. These were impressive as hell. State-of-the-art Soviet jobs, they were designated by the Russian weapon manufacturers as the M1937 medium mortar. They lobbed 82-millimeter shells that could be delivered at a rate of between fifteen and twenty-five rounds per minute. The maximum range of the weapons was a bit over 3,000 meters with a minimum of 100. Since the Black Eagles were dug in 700 meters from the NVA heavy weapons company, the Red gunners would have no problem finding the target.

The crews, well-drilled and practiced, set up the weapons, laid them in on the aiming stakes, then waited for the orders to start dropping shells down the tubes.

It wasn't long coming.

The first explosions — a series of six — gushed out in overwhelming roars of orange flashes and black, dense smoke. The Black Eagles, down deep in their previously prepared fighting holes, could only grit their teeth and endure the pounding concussion that seemed to pull the breath from their lungs. The barrage went on for a full half hour before it let up. If anyone had bothered to count, they would have discovered there had been a total of almost five hundred leisurely fired rounds delivered onto their positions.

The silence following the bombardment seemed as loud as the explosions.

Falconi's men knew this pause did not mean a respite in the fighting. The NVA infantry would move in quickly after the bombardment to take advantage of the shock effect such shelling produces in its victims.

But they hadn't reckoned on the extraordinary guts and esprit-de-corps of the Black Eagles. When a group of hairy-eared bastards will not accept the fact they can be beaten, they will take a considerable amount of convincing to make them think otherwise. That mortar barrage obviously wasn't enough.

The enemy infantry burst out of the jungle emitting their battle cries. Full of their commissars' harangues and egged on by the officers and NCOs, these young riflemen were primed for a quick victory.

The volleys from the Black Eagles' positions may have been from light weapons, but they were devastating. Semi-automatic fire was combined with full-automatic to sweep the area ahead in overlapping waves of carefully aimed and placed fusillades. The front line of the attackers were swept away to the last man. The second group lasted a bit longer—at least to the point of being stopped—but still could boast of no survivors. The following skirmishers were also brought to a staggering halt, but enough were alive to be able to pull off a respectable retrograde movement under the careful guidance of their leaders.

The mortar barrage was repeated.

Falconi and his men pressed themselves into the dirt floors of their fighting positions as the overwhelming thundering shook the ground and sent showers of dirt and rock up in the air to fall back down on them.

This time the NVA were so anxious to attack that they jumped the gun a bit. Their lead attackers were not wiped out by the Black Eagles. Instead, their own mortar shells blew them to pieces as they charged into the hell of the final spasms of exploding rounds.

The full brunt of Black Eagle defensive firing was again blasted at the enemy who stormed out of the jungle. The NVA officers were hoping to use the advantage of their superior numbers to sweep over the Americans, so they urged more and more platoons into the fight.

The poor, dumb bastards broke their hearts as 5.56 millimeter bullets and rifle grenades mowed them down like stalks of wheat hit by a scythe. It is to the Reds' credit that they continued the assault as bodies of their dead and wounded piled up in a pathetic line of corpses that stretched across the entire width of that side of the village.

They withdrew again. This time in confused, unco-ordinated spasms of retreat that broke up organizational integrity and added to the difficulty for small unit commanders to maintain any leadership or control.

Quiet replaced the thundering roar of rifle fire.

Lt. Col. Robert Falconi licked at the sweat on his upper lip. "If those goddamned mortars don't get us, we could hold onto this village 'til hell freezes over."

"Yes, sir," Chief Brewster agreed from over in his own fighting hole. He pulled a fresh group of magazines out of his ammo pouches and laid them on the poncho at his feet so they would be easier to reach. "I'm afraid we'll wear these damned weapons out before this thing is over."

"They're really heated up," Falconi admitted. "But not enough to make any difference now."

The silence continued for several more minutes, then was broken by the militia captain's shouting voice. "*Trung-ta* Falconi!"

"Yes. Over here," Falconi said loudly with gestures.

Trang raced across a short open space and dove into the lieutenant colonel's hole. He wasted no time in speaking out what was on his mind. "I need attack from you, *Trung-ta*. There is a place the villagers can get through and out into the jungle. But you must draw the NVA away first."

Falconi had promised to help the people of Tam Nuroc, but he wanted no sacrifice to be in vain. "What is the probability of success, Captain Trang?"

"Excellent!" Trang said. "The Reds do not expect much action to the south. They have troops there. If you attack to the north—on the riverfront—it will cause them to shift their lines. It leaves a wide path open for the people to flee through."

What Trang was suggesting would mean that the

Black Eagles must leave their safe fighting holes and face an overwhelming number of NVA in the open. That gave Falconi some food for thought. If such an attack went to the river, they might as well try to steal a couple of boats. The chances were slim to nil since the detachment wasn't armed properly for such a wild undertaking, and they would be exposed to flanking fire that could sweep them away like dead leaves before a gusty autumn wind.

Nevertheless, it was a chance of sorts.

"We'll do it," Falconi said. "I'll give you fifteen minutes to prepare the people. At that time we'll move forward."

Trang's eyes watered with emotion and his lips trembled. "You are brave! The risk is great."

"We'll get to the boats and pull a—" Falconi laughed. "A—strategic withdrawal."

"I go, *Trung-ta*. Thank you! Thank you!" With little time to spare, Trang rushed off to tend to the task of preparing the group of civilians for a wild rush to safety.

Falconi summoned his team leaders, Chris Hawkins and Ray Swift Elk, and gave them their simple orders. Move forward and fight like hell to the river. Once there, play it by ear, but get into the nearest boats and haul ass.

Like Trang, the Black Eagles couldn't tarry. Within five minutes of issuing the team leaders their orders, both the Alphas and Bravos were ready to go.

Ray Swift Elk, with the Bravos, checked his men. He could see Calvin Culpepper down on his left, and Blue Richards on his right. He stood up to check Malpractice McCorckel, but could see nothing. "Hey, Blue!" he yelled. "Where's Malpractice at?"

"I'll check," Blue hollered back. "He can't have gone far. He was right beside me when you issued

207

them orders." The Alabama sailor disappeared through the village huts, then returned. His face wore a puzzled expression. "Damn, Ray! He's gone! Disappeared! I can't see him nowheres."

Before Swift Elk could react to the news, Falconi yelled his commands and the Black Eagles left their fighting holes to sweep forward in the desperate attack.

Second Lieutenant Betty Lou Pemberton moved slowly down the row of beds holding the wounded soldiers. The army nurse, stationed in Long Binh, worked in the surgical recovery ward where the injured and maimed convalesced from their operations and treatment to either be sent back to the World, or returned to their units for more combat.

She was looking for a particular patient, and slowly read the name cards on the bedrails. Finally she found the man she was looking for. The nurse walked around the bed and approached him. She smiled at the rough looking old soldier who lay there on the sheets. "I hear they call you 'Top'."

Top Gordon looked up at her and instantly noticed her big tits. He grinned. "That's me, Lieutenant."

"I have a special someone in your unit," Betty Lou said. "In fact," she added pointing down the row of beds. "I met him right down there."

Top then knew who she was. "You're Archie Dobbs' girl, ain't you?"

Betty Lou nodded. "I sure am." The expression on her face became more serious. "How is he doing?"

"The last time I seen Archie, he was sitting on a river dock smoking a cigarette and waving bye-bye to me as my evacuation chopper lifted off," Top said. "Don't worry about that guy, Lieutenant. He'll take care of himself."

"That's quite an outfit you're in, Top," Betty Lou said. "The ward doctor tells me you were operated on by your medic." She laughed. "I'd already heard about the guy from Archie. He described him as a rather strongwilled individual who goes by the rather alarming name of 'Malpractice'."

"Archie must have told you about all of us."

"He sure did," the nurse said. She unbuttoned Top's pajama jacket and opened the garment. She raised the bandages a bit to check the wound. "Does that hurt?"

"Not a bit."

"I still find it hard to believe that an enlisted medic actually cut into you, reached below and behind your heart, removed a bullet there, then sewed you up."

Top laughed lightly. "I just hope the arrogant sonofabitch doesn't send me a bill!"

"Really? What's the going rate among Black Eagles for saving each other's lives?" Betty Lou asked.

"A beer — not a word spoken — just a nice cold beer and a pat on the back," Top said. "Let me tell you something, Lieutenant. That's worth more than the Medal of Honor."

"To you guys it probably is," the nurse said. "By the way — call me Betty Lou."

"Sure," Top said.

"I hope you don't mind me calling you 'Top'."

"O'course not! You're practically one o' the family, Betty Lou."

"In that case, is there anything I can get for you?" she asked.

"Speaking of cases — that much beer would be nice."

But Betty Lou shook her head in a definitely negative manner. "You're still under too much seda-

209

tion for alcohol, Top. That was a serious operation you had. It'll be a while before you're ready to get back to normal."

"I'll behave if you promise me a case of Budweiser when I'm pronounced fit for duty," Top said.

"It's a promise."

"Jesus, little lady, I can see why Archie fell for you," Top said with a wink.

"I'm an All-American girl," Betty Lou said with a laugh. "Now relax and get some more sleep, Top. You're in for a lengthy recovery." She walked away, pausing only to add, "Sweet dreams."

"Thanks," Top said. He turned his thoughts back to the detachment, and his mood grew somber. If Betty Lou Pemberton knew the shit her boyfriend was in, there'd be no sweet dreams for her.

The Black Eagles' assault caught the NVA flat-footed.

Their mortar crews had gone back to the river to unload more ammunition and lug it back to their firing position. The Reds' orders still stood. There would be numerous barrages from the heavy weapons into the village, that would be interrupted with infantry attacks.

None of their officers had figured the crazy bastards in the village would attack them.

The Black Eagle assault first swept over the thin picket posts set out in front of the main position. Then they hit the enemy's MLR—Main Line of Resistance—and the momentum of their storm tactics carried them completely through even these well prepared positions.

NVA died in mute surprise as they were hosed by the Black Eagles' M16s. Falconi, being the best

210

runner in the detachment, was the first to hit the docks. The NVA commander's headquarters was there and his staff, just as shocked as their men, took casualties that pitched forward over map tables or staggered back to fall into the river to make bloody splashes in the muddy water.

There was no time to be choosy. There was only one of their own boats available. Falconi had hoped to be able to latch onto one of the NVA's heavier armed launches, but these were on the other side of the waterfront. The lieutenant colonel leaped aboard and went directly to the control console to punch the craft's engines into life.

Chris Hawkins and Ray Swift Elk had kept complete control of their respective teams. They immediately stopped the charge when it reached the docks. Their men turned around and delivered covering fire back into the weak attack of Reds that had been hastily and desperately mounted against them.

"Into the boat!" Falconi yelled.

One more wild-assed volley, and the detachment crowded aboard. Falconi pushed forward on the throttle and cranked the wheel. The launch wheeled in the water, throwing out a wild wake, and headed for the middle of the river.

But all hopes of escape were dashed when three NVA boats, their heavy machine guns firing, swept out to intercept them. The big 12.7 millimeter rounds smacked, splattered and rocked the craft slapping gaping holes into the gunwales and across the foredeck.

"Oh, shit!" Archie exclaimed. "I'm glad we can all swim!"

Blue Richards, spraying full-auto fire at the NVA boats, was more pessimistic. "Just how goddamned far do you think they'll let us get?"

Then the control console exploded in front of Falconi's face as a half dozen of the big slugs blasted it apart.

From all appearances, the Battle of Tam Nuroc was over — and the defeat promised watery graves for the Black Eagles.

CHAPTER 20

Malpractice McCorckel and Jean were late in getting out of the village.

When the main group of villagers fled under the leadership of Captain Trang and the local militia, she had hung back hoping to at least be able to have a short farewell with her lover. But she'd tarried too long, and when the Black Eagle assault was launched, the beautiful young Vietnamese woman figured Malpractice had also gone with them. By the time she turned back to join the other civilians, they were already gone.

Jean, in fear, had rushed into the jungle to hide. Her best opportunity for survival would be to find a good place to conceal herself. If the Black Eagles were victorious, she could emerge when they returned. If not, she would have to stay out of sight and either escape when the NVA troops were less alert, or wait until they withdrew completely from Tam Nuroc. She knew if the Reds found her, and any turncoats or collaborators living in Tam Nuroc identified her as not only working with the Americans, but sleeping with one, the Communists would be quick to show that being friendly with their enemies was a fatal mistake.

Malpractice's own situation began when the order to attack was given. The briefing that Ray Swift Elk had given him and the other two members of Bravo Fire Team, had informed him of the villagers' withdrawal. He was already in a mixed up emotional state, and the thought of Jean being in danger pushed him over the deep end.

He did the one thing no soldier is ever supposed to do: he left his post during a battle.

It took the intrepid medic almost an hour of frantic searching before he found the young woman. He had at first rushed off to join the villagers and fight alongside the militia, but when he discovered that Jean wasn't with them, he'd turned back to search for her. He knew she would do the smart thing and hide in the jungle, so he rushed around the outskirts of the village calling her name. When Jean finally heard him, she quickly answered.

Their reunion was made up of a quick embrace and Jean's tears of relief that the man she loved was safe. Malpractice couldn't waste a lot of time on sentiments. "We won't be able to rejoin the villagers and the militia," he told Jean. "They're too far away by this time."

"I was going to hide in the jungle," Jean said. "Perhaps we should go back to where I was when you called."

"That's the only choice we've got now," Malpractice said. "But we've got to get even farther away. The NVA has mortars and they might decide to chew up the surrounding area with some barrages in case there

214

are people out there." He had an aggressive nature, and preferred to meet his adversaries head-on. But there was a logical side to him too, particularly when Jean's safety depended on the course of action he chose.

They moved swiftly and silently through the clinging vegetation, seeking to penetrate deeper into the green sanctuary where they could hole up. Malpractice had everything with him they would need if an extensive and long journey of escape and evasion should become necessary. His survival kit went beyond the regular knife, fish hooks, snares, special rations and other tools. The medic also had drugs and medicines to help them along. There were pills and capsules to keep awake, or sleep; to stay alert, or relax; defecate or stop diarrhea; and others to take care of the countless physical problems that crop up when one is surviving off the land and nature. He also had a dozen special ones sealed in a small tin can which guaranteed instantaneous and painless death.

But he had nothing that would help the situation they stumbled into after an hour's travel.

The black pajama clad Viet Cong soldiers appeared from nowhere. Armed with AK47s, these were farm boys, uneducated and steeped with Communist propaganda of the most violent nature. They immediately recognized they had an American soldier at their mercy.

Normally, Malpractice would have hosed them away and taken his chance. But Jean was with him, and he was more concerned about her safety than his own. He threw the M16 into the jungle and raised his hands. *"Toi muon hang di!"*

The lead VC snarled and raised his weapon speaking the only words he knew in English: "American die!"

Then he squeezed the trigger.

Falconi lost control of the boat and it spun around with the throttle locked wide-open.

More fusillades of heavy machine gun fire slammed into the wildly careening craft while the Black Eagles aboard tried to return fire. What volleys they could muster were ill-aimed and weak.

Then the motor was hit and the craft suddenly stopped and settled in the water. The NVA launches sped toward them. The Black Eagles, if they were to die, would do so fighting.

Paulo and Calvin fired off grenades with the M203s as fast as the single-shot arrangement would permit. The rest of the detachment zapped full-automatic fire at the charging enemy.

Then suddenly the leading boat in the enemy attack blew apart.

Falconi, suddenly aware of firing from another direction, snapped his head around and saw a South Vietnamese boat speeding into the battle. There was a quad-fifty mounted on it, and the weapon was firing in efficient bursts that were accurate and knocking hell out of the attacking craft.

Calvin Culpepper shoved another 40-millimeter grenade into his weapon. "Hey! Is that ol' Fagin there?"

Ray Swift Elk, his copper-colored features sweat-streaked, laughed aloud. "It sure as hell is!"

One more launch armed with a quad-fifty swept into the battle while yet another friendly boat came alongside. The Black Eagles recognized the ARVN officer from Dak Bla. "Would you like please to come onto my boat to which you are most welcome?" he asked. "For I have observed that the boat of yourselves is fast going lower and lower into the water."

By that time all the attacking NVA boats were shot to splinters. The pounding from Fagin's quad-fifties had done them in. The bodies of dead and wounded crewmen floated in the reddening turbulence of the Song Cai.

Now the CIA officer and the other ARVN boat were gleefully sweeping Tam Nuroc's docks with the fifty-caliber fire.

Falconi turned to the South Vietnamese major and ordered him to take his men in to assault the village. "There's mortars in there," he told him. "If they turn those babies around, this battle ends now with us all dead."

"Please not to worry," the officer said. "My brave men and I shall go forth to wipe out the surviving enemies."

The final spasms of the battle were short and merciful. The NVA commander Ngy was dead. His surviving officers surrendered the men who could not flee the devastating fire and subsequent infantry assault of the combined Black Eagle and ARVN forces.

The prisoners, dazed from the unexpected attack Falconi and his men had launched out of the village, then hit hard by both the heavy quad-fifties and the reinforcements of South Vietnamese infantry, held their hands high as they were roughly searched. Then they were shoved into a growing crowd guarded by the guns of victory-flushed ARVN soldiers.

The reunion with Fagin could only be described as one of those love/hate situations.

And the CIA man played it for all it was worth. He stood up on the foredeck leaning nonchalantly on the four-machine gun contraption he'd brought with him as his boat drew alongside the dock. He had a stogie in his mouth, that he casually chewed on as if he were coming in from a fishing trip.

When the launch was stopped, he walked over and leaped off. Falconi and all his men were standing there. Sweat-streaked, dirty and near exhaustion from the long hours of fighting, they were a marked contrast to how dapper Fagin appeared.

Falconi, his M16 slung over his right shoulder, stood with his arms folded across his chest. "Welcome to Tam Nuroc."

"Thanks, pal," Falconi said. "I heard you were having a little difficulty, so I thought I'd come up and pull your silly asses out of all the shit you were in."

Archie Dobbs wasn't amused. "You mean all the shit you put us in, asshole!"

"Oh, my, Archie!" Fagin said feigning shock. "You're so crude when you get emotional."

Archie snarled. "I'm emotional enough to kick your ass!"

"You try it, shorty," Fagin snapped back, "I'll hit you so hard on top of the head you'll have to unbutton your shirt to see."

"Ho! Ho! That's rich!" Archie said unable to think of a good comeback. He also knew that Fagin could whip him soundly on any given day.

"You two schoolboys knock that shit off," Falconi said in disgust. "Jesus Christ! What a couple of bad-asses."

Chris Hawkins reported in after bringing the Alpha Team together. "Sir, we're all present and accounted for. No casualties."

"Great," Falconi snapped. He looked over where the prisoners were still being searched and shoved around in a most ungentle manner. Ray Swift Elk emerged from the village huts with Paulo and Blue following him. His face was grim. Falconi waited for him to walk up. "What's happening with your team?"

"We can't find Malpractice," Swift Elk said. "There's no body—nothing."

Archie's anger at Fagin faded away and was replaced by grief. He squatted down and hung his head. "Oh, man. Not ol' Malpractice!"

"There has to be a cadaver," Paulo said.

But Blue Richards shook his head. As a demolitions specialist, he knew the effect of explosions on humans. "Not if one o' them mortar rounds found him, man. A direct hit would turn him into atoms. They wouldn't be nothing left."

Fagin, too, was saddened. "He was one of the original of the group, wasn't he?"

"Yeah," Falconi said. "It looks like the only people left from the old sweats are Calvin Culpepper and me now."

Blue looked down at Archie. "Wasn't you one o' the first'uns in the Black Eagles?"

"Naw," Archie said standing up again. "I came in on the second mission." He smiled weakly at Falconi. "The Falcon there dragged me out of a Saigon whorehouse. I joined Malpractice then. There was other guys that are gone too. Lightfingers O'Quinn, Horny Galchaser, Top Snow—"

"Knock it off, Archie!" Falconi snapped. "I've already been through that with Malpractice. I don't need more of it."

Archie, shocked, almost leaped into the position of attention. "Yes, sir!"

"We've got things to do before we wrap up this mission," Falconi said. He looked around for Chief Brewster. "Hey, Chief!"

"Yes, sir?"

"Contact Abner," he said referring to the radio call sign of operations headquarters. "Tell them we've brought Operation Song Cai to a successful conclusion. And have them pass the word that there's be a couple of hundred POWs available to G2 for questioning."

"Aye, aye, sir!" The chief disappeared into the headquarters hut to crank up the AN/PRC-41 radio.

Ray Swift Elk turned Calvin and Blue over to the Alphas for the necessary work details and clean-up that would be necessary before they withdrew from Tam Nuroc and began the return trip to Nui Dep. He tapped Falconi on the shoulder. "We gotta talk, sir. S2 business."

Falconi was puzzled. "Hell, there's nothing left to do but write up the intelligence annex to the after-action report."

"There's some loose threads," the Sioux Indian said. "I want to know how come that frigging whorehouse lady didn't get the word to us about the NVA steaming toward the village here. And if she did try to send a warning, I want to know what happened."

Fagin was listening to the exchange. "That's my department too," he said.

Swift Elk snapped his piercing eyes in the direction of the CIA officer. "*You* were the one that set us up with the bitch!"

Fagin almost protested about being as surprised with the lady as an asset too, but he remembered his philosophy of having the Black Eagles hate him personally for the fuckups. It was easier on them that way, than if they knew there were other powers that played fast and loose with their safety. So he kept calm. "Then, Ray, it really makes sense to let me in on the investigation, doesn't it?"

"Okay," Falconi said. "Both you guys pay a visit to her."

"I hope you haven't developed any fondness for the

lady," Fagin said. "If it turns out she's a double-agent, I'll have to off her."

"That's your style," Archie said from a distance. "Shooting a broad."

"Yeah," Fagin said with a grin. He pulled his .45 from the shoulder holster he sported. "Hey, are there any little kids—sick ones, that is—around here that I can shoot, huh? Please, fellows?"

"That ain't funny, Fagin," Swift Elk said in disgust. But he knew the man was right about Fleurette Hue:

There was a good chance the lady had to die.

The bullets whizzed around Malpractice. He shoved violently against Jean, pushing her into the bushes off the narrow trail where they'd been standing. He fully expected to feel the first impacts of the rounds, and he instinctively closed his eyes tight as the shooting continued.

But, somehow, he was unharmed. He took a quick look and saw the three VC lying dead in front of him.

"Howdy, Malpractice."

The medic jerked around in startled surprise to find both Erick Stensland and Gunnar the Gunner Olson stepping out onto the jungle track.

"Damn," Stensland said. "We've had a hell of a time this week. We've been evading the goddamned VC and trying to get to Tam Nuroc, but there's been traffic up and down the river and more damned Reds running through this jungle until it was like Grand Central Station."

"They're all dead," Gunnar said after inspecting the cadavers.

Jean, recognizing the two by the uniforms they wore, rejoined Malpractice. She clung tightly to him and only managed a half smile when she was introduced.

"Do you have any family lost or unaccounted for, Miss?" Stensland asked.

"No. They are all with the militia," Jean answered.

"We found a dead kid," Gunnar said.

"Yeah," Stensland added, "and he had a note on him. I only recognize the word *americain*. I remember from my French class at good ol' Knee Lake High School that the word means 'American'. This could be a message for Falconi."

"We'll find out soon enough," Malpractice said. "Let's head back for the village. If our boys have carried the day, we'll rejoin them. If not—" He let it hang.

"More escape-and-evasion," Stensland said with a sigh. He glanced at Gunnar. "Ain't that a bitch?"

Gunnar the Gunner shrugged. "I don't know. This kind o' country is interesting. Nothing at all like Minnesota."

"Gunnar!" Stensland exclaimed. "Even if you are a shirt-tail relative, you're still a crazy Norwegian sonofabitch!"

CHAPTER 21

Archie Dobbs sat nonchalantly on the porch of the headquarters hutch. He absent-mindedly cleaned his fingernails with his bayonet as he watched the recently arrived visitor walk up the village street toward him.

This was the agent Choy. As usual, he had been out in the jungle for a long time on one of his clandestine reconnaisance missions. Disheveled and worn out, he moved slowly with a great deal of effort. His physical appearance was that of a man who had recently been deprived of civilization's comforts. But his face formed a smile—though a weary one—for Archie. He walked up to the Black Eagle scout. "How you, Archie? Okie-dokie?"

Archie grinned back at him. "Hell, yes, Choy. You look like you was the only one who showed up at an ax fight without an ax. Where've you been?"

"Out in deep, hot jungle," Choy said. "Try to find VC. When find VC, wait to see what they do. Lot of walk and hide. This is tough life, Archie." He looked around at the bullet-pocked village. "Look like village catch hell, Archie."

"We had a big battle," Archie remarked.

"Ah! I know," Choy said sitting down beside him. "I was up north when I hear of retreat of NVA river unit. I go and see for myself. Sure enough, they all tore up. Lose lots of mans, and lots captured too."

"You bet," Archie said cheerfully. "We kicked their asses all right."

"Oh, yes, very much," Choy agreed.

"I think the Falcon wants to see you inside," Archie said gesturing toward the door. "He said if you showed up, to tell you to go on in. I don't know if it's important or not, but maybe you should see him before you eat or anything."

"Sure," Choy said. There was something disturbing about Archie's relaxed mood that bothered the agent. But he couldn't quite figure out what it was. He laboriously got to his feet. "I know what he want. Count of enemy survivors. Not very many. That what I will tell him."

Archie laughed. "Okay. See you later, Choy."

"Okay, Archie." The Chinese-Vietnamese went to the door and rapped on it. He stepped inside.

Falconi sat at his desk. He looked up from the after-action report he was working on. "Hello, Choy. We're happy to see you."

"Me too," Choy said.

Fagin stood off to one side. He smiled at Choy, then slowly pulled the .45 auto from the tanker shoulder holster under his shirt. He aimed the pistol straight on the agent. "Freeze, you motherfucker!"

"Hey. No game, eh?" Choy said angrily. "That thing loaded?"

"As sure as whores fuck," Fagin said ominously.

Ray Swift Elk spoke from the opposite side of the room. "This ain't a game. Get your hands up."

Choy instantly obeyed. "What the matter, eh?"

224

"First we check you out for weapons," Fagin said. "Strip."

Choy hesitated, but the genuine threat in the pair's voices told him not to anger them. "This is not way to do a friend," he said in way of a diplomatic protest. He slowly stepped out of his clothing until he was naked.

"The sandals too," Swift Elk said.

Choy kicked them off. "I want to know what wrong, okay? You tell me."

Fagin ignored the request. He walked up to him and checked his armpits, crotch and mouth. "Bend over."

"Okay! Okay! I do." Choy did as he was told.

Fagin looked up his ass. "Okay, fuckface. Pull it out."

Choy deftly withdrew the capsule from his rectum. "Nothing in it," he said. "I all the time have for carry secret message."

"Open it," Fagin said.

Choy opened the smelly, vaseline coated container. "See. It empty."

Swift Elk's Indian features were menacing. "We been talking to Fleurette Hue."

"Ah! No good whore," Choy said. "Lie too much."

"No," Fagin said. "She didn't lie. As a matter of fact she put a lot of notes at that deadletter drop that never got to us."

Choy looked at Falconi. "Get them off my back, okay? Fucking whore lie."

Falconi got up and sauntered to the door. He paused, and turned to speak. "I'd say you're in a bit of trouble."

Choy's face was distorted with fear. "I tell you she lie. No notes in deadletter drop. Never."

Falconi warned him, "You'd better be damned

convincing to those two, Choy." He gave the agent the meaningful glance before he left.

Choy repeated his protest. "The whore lie!"

"She sent a note with her houseboy, Choy," Fagin said. "But somebody killed him."

Swift Elk snarled, "But the killer didn't search the body. The piece of paper was in the little guy's pants pocket."

"I don't know nothing," Choy said sullenly.

"We think you killed the boy," Fagin said. "Evidently you thought he was bringing a verbal message to Falconi."

"What is *verbal*?" Choy asked.

Swift Elk's finger tightened in the trigger, then relaxed. "That means you thought he had something to *tell* Falconi."

"Right," Fagin echoed. "You didn't know she'd written the note and the kid had it in his pocket."

"She not write fucking note!" Choy protested.

"It's in her handwriting, asshole," Swift Elk said. "We checked that out. And if she wasn't sending anything in the deadletter drop, why would she suddenly send us a note saying that the NVA were approaching Tam Nuroc?" Swift Elk paused and studied Choy's face. "That puts you in a bad light, don't it, Choy?"

Choy gulped and sucked in his breath. He felt cold, stabbing fear as his instinct for survival set every nerve in his body on edge.

"You're in a peculiar situation, Choy," Fagin said calmly. "There's a big cloud of doubt hanging over you. We've got no choice but to kill you."

Choy thought fast. The CIA man was right. Any mistrust or even the slightest taint on an agent's reputation was tantamount to a death sentence. He had to come up with something quick to save his ass.

226

It had to be something that would make him more valuable alive than dead, and he had to be truthful about it. "Okay. Okay. I tell you something."

"We're waiting, asshole," Swift Elk said.

"I—uh," he stammered in hesitation. Then suddenly, he blurted out, "I a double-agent."

"Lying motherfucker!" Fagin shouted. "Don't insult our intelligence." He aimed the pistol straight at Choy's face.

Choy shuddered with fright. "No shoot! No shoot!" Tears came to his eyes and his voice quaked. "The Reds call me Tho May. I can give you much information—many names and places where agents who work for the communists are."

"You just might save your ass, Choy," Fagin said. "That is, if you start talking fast and convincingly."

Choy, alias Tho May, began doing exactly that.

CHAPTER 22

The hangar at the airbase Chu Lai was much cooler than the sunbaked runways outside. The Black Eagles sprawled in the large building next to the C-130 that was scheduled to fly them back to Camp Nui Dep later that same afternoon.

Falconi, Chris Hawkins and Swift Elk huddled together off to one side of the group. As the leaders, they had the usual administrative problems and details to unsnarl after a mission. The trio was in one hell of a good mood.

The mission had been accomplished, and the Song Cai River now belonged to South Vietnam again. But the best thing was that there had not been a single KIA among them. While it was true that Sergeant Major Gordon had been wounded, they had received the word from the U.S. Army Hospital at Long Binh, that he was well onto the road to recovery and would be able to rejoin the unit after a bit of convalescence.

Part of their impromptu meeting in the hangar had been to discuss the one question that had been bugging both Falconi and Swift Elk throughout the mission.

This had involved Malpractice McCorckel's deteriorating morale. It would be a near insult to place him on a rest leave. But there was no doubt the medic was in bad need of a long break from combat.

Finally, through Chris Hawkin's efforts, a solution had been reached.

They walked back to the main group. Falconi looked over at both Malpractice McCorckel and Calvin Culpepper. "You two guys get over to the MATS office and find Fagin. You'll be flying out with him."

"What for, Falcon?" Calvin asked. "He's got guards for Choy—or Tho May or whatever the motherfucker's name is—from the Air Police."

"Yeah," Malpractice said. "He don't need us."

"You won't be doing anything with Fagin," Falconi said. "Both of you guys have now racked up ten missions with the detachment. You're the old sweats."

Malpractice lit a cigarette. "Are we gonna get some extra R&R, sir?"

"Both of you are getting thirty day furloughs," Falconi said, "and another thirty days of administrative leave on top of that."

"Sixty days!" Calvin exclaimed.

Even Malpractice brightened a bit.

"You'll be getting open-ended papers that'll let you go anywhere you want," Falconi said.

Malpractice showed his usual concern for others. "Hell, sir! What about you? You've had eleven trips out into hell."

Falconi grinned and shrugged. He patted the maple leaf on his collar that indicated his rank of lieutenant colonel. "It's lonely at the top, guys."

Calvin suddenly jumped up and grabbed his gear. "Damn, Malpractice! Let's get on over to the MATS office. That fuckin' Fagin might leave without us."

Malpractice joined him, but moved a lot slower. "I still say you need some time off, too."

Falconi smiled. "Thanks, Malpractice. I'll manage."

"Damn right you will," Malpractice said. He waved at the others and trotted off after Calvin.

Archie Dobbs watched them disappear across the air base. Then he looked at Falconi. "So our next mission will be without them two, huh?" he said. "I've never gone into combat as a Black Eagle without Malpractice and Calvin."

Falconi saw the aircraft crew coming into the large hangar. "Don't worry about it," he said. "Anyhow, here comes the airplane driver. Let's get our stuff aboard."

The men hustled to get on the C-130. Within ten minutes after settling in, the big airplane rolled out of the hangar onto the runway. After a warm-up, it raced faster and faster down the concrete until it lifted slowly and majestically into the air.

Falconi turned in the webbed seat and looked out the small porthole beside him. He watched Chu Lai slide past them, then looked outward.

The Song Cai River, muddy and deep, snaked through the bright green of the jungle. It looked insignificant and even a bit worthless. Particularly to people who didn't know about the bones of dead soldiers that now littered the silty bottom.

The lieutenant colonel straightened up and glanced at the men in the fuselage with him. They were already stretched out on the floor and falling into cat naps.

Like tigers, he thought, returning to their lair before the next foray to the outside to hunt and kill.

Calcitra clunis.

230

Now there was nothing to worry about. No guards to post, no potential attack to prepare for, and no double-agent to betray the Black Eagles.

Their world, for a while at any rate, was at peace.

Falconi leaned back and closed his own eyes, to drift off into a deep, dreamless sleep.

EPILOGUE

Marcel Leroux liked working with the Americans. As an officer in the French army he'd never known the luxuries and comforts that most of the *americaines* seemed to take for granted. He'd put in thirty-five years of service before retiring with the rank of *general de brigade*. His crowning success in the military had not been in a victory like World War II, but in the defeat in Indo-China.

Leroux had organized and led a select group of men known by the rather unimpressive title of G.M.I. These were the French initials for several units listed as Composite Intervention Groups. These were made up of specially selected ass-kickers and trouble-makers among the officers and sergeants, who went out into the Indo-Chinese boondocks to recruit, train and lead native guerrillas. This activity developed into some of the dirtiest partisan activity imaginable.

The G.M.I.s were quite successful within their small sphere, but without good support and backing they were doomed to failure. Some returned after the armistice, but many were left in unmarked jungle graves to be listed on the rolls of the army as *Perdu-de-la-Guerre* — Missing-In-Action.

General Leroux retired from the military in the early 1960s. He moved into a rather staid life on some family property out in the country south of Paris. He'd been rescued from this boring existence by the American CIA. The general was well known to several top officials of that American intelligence agency, and they recruited him to work for them. Although this required his return to Vietnam, he was to act in a purely advisory capacity in a program quit similar to his old G.MI. These operations were carried out by units of the United States Army's Green Berets.

He was provided with a nice apartment in Saigon and worked at Peterson Field where the Special Operations Group had their headquarters.

He had just finished work one evening and was on his way to join some American friends at the Ton Son Nhut main officers club when a young SOG captain approached him in the hall.

"I beg your pardon, General," the captain said. "I wonder if I could ask a favor of you."

"Certainement, Capitaine," General Leroux said courteously.

"We have been receiving a voice radio broadcast for the past several months," the captain said. "It is very weak and sounds like it is French."

"I would be most 'appy to listen to it for you,"

234

General Leroux said in his heavy accent. Although his English was perfect, he'd never been able to master the pronunciation properly.

The captain was apologetic as he led the general to the communications room. "This is probably a waste of your time, but it's been bothering me for quite some time. It just started up again, and I rushed out here to find you."

They went to a large receiving set where a sergeant sat working the dials. The captain tapped him on the shoulder. "Put it on the speaker."

"Yes, sir."

There was a continuous crackling sound, but behind this audio disturbance, a man's voice could easily be heard.

"Niche. Niche. C'est Chien. A vous. Niche. C'est Chien. A vous."

Leroux stared incredulously at the radio. Suddenly, after the speaker repeated the call several more times, he grabbed a microphone. *"Chien. C'est Niche. Pourquoi ecorcez-vous? A vous."*

There was a hesitation, but the voice came back and the emotion in it was undeniable. The man was almost shouting in a frenzy. *"Je ne ecorce pas! Je morde!"*

The French general's hands shook, and he looked in wide-eyed wonder at the captain. The American officer was alarmed. "Jesus, sir! What's the matter!"

"That man on the radio, 'e 'as just given the proper identification of the G.M.I. — *Groupement Mixte d'Intervention* — as a French guerrilla leader from our war here."

"You mean the poor bastard has been out there in the jungle fighting the French-Indochinese War all

235

this time?" the captain wondered.

Leroux held out his hands in a gesture of wonderment. "That man, a French officer or sergeant, has been serving *en combat* for at least fifteen years!"